EASTERN MOUNTAINS

RAT CREATURE TEMPLE

CONKLE'S HOLLOW

UPPER PAWA

PAWA

FLINT RIDGE

THE GREAT BASIN

TANEN GARD

PRAYER STONE HILL

PAWA ROAD

ATHEIA

GULCH

SINNER'S ROCK

THE SAGA CONTINUES

BY JEFF SMITH

WITH COLOUR BY STEVE HAMAKER

Scholastic Canada Ltd.
Toronto New York London Auckland Sydney
Mexico City New Delhi Hong Kong Buenos Aires

Scholastic Canada Ltd.
604 King Street West, Toronto, Ontario M5V 1E1, Canada

Scholastic Inc.
557 Broadway, New York, NY 10012, USA

Scholastic Australia Pty Limited
PO Box 579, Gosford, NSW 2250, Australia

Scholastic New Zealand Limited
Private Bag 94407, Botany, Manukau 2163, New Zealand

Scholastic Children's Books
Euston House, 24 Eversholt Street, London NW1 1DB, UK

ACKNOWLEDGMENTS
Harvestar Family Crest designed by Charles Vess
Map of The Valley by Mark Crilley
Color by Steve Hamaker

Book design by David Saylor

ISBN 978-1-4431-1306-9

6 5 4 3 2 1   Printed in Singapore 46   11 12 13 14 15

CONTENTS

This book is for Irene Kilty

for inspiring her grandson's imagination

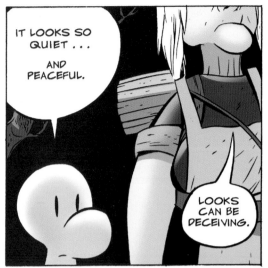

IT LOOKS SO QUIET...

AND PEACEFUL.

LOOKS CAN BE DECEIVING.

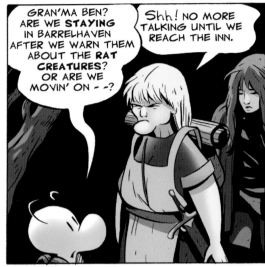

GRAN'MA BEN? ARE WE **STAYING** IN BARRELHAVEN AFTER WE WARN THEM ABOUT THE **RAT CREATURES**? OR ARE WE MOVIN' ON – –?

Shh! NO MORE TALKING UNTIL WE REACH THE INN.

WE'RE NOT OUT OF TH' WOODS YET.

CAN'T ARGUE WITH **THAT.**

SO WHAT **HAPPENED**?

BY TH' TIME TANNER GOT OUT TO THE **SHED**, TH' DRAGON WAS **GONE**!

HOWDY, **FELLAS**! ANOTHER ROUND?

SURE, BONE!

HOW 'BOUT YOU, MR. EUCLID?

YEAH! AN' BRING US SOME OF THOSE HARD, STUFFED, LITTLE **BREAD THINGIES** YOU'RE SO GOOD AT MAKIN'!

SMILEY! MORE ALE OVER HERE!

ANOTHER ROUND -- **COMIN' UP**! NEED ANY LITTLE THING FROM TH' **KITCHEN**? CHEF PHONEY AWAITS YOUR ORDERS!

YEAH, GIMME TH' **DRAGONSLAYER** SPECIAL!

FLAME-BROILED CHICKEN! YOU GOT IT! BE RIGHT BACK!

. . . THEN **I** SAY, TH' BEST THING YOU CAN **DO** AT NIGHT IS KEEP YOUR FAMILY **INDOORS**!

RIGHT! YOU'RE **RIGHT**! YOU CAN'T BE TOO **CAREFUL** WITH THIS **DRAGON** PROBLEM . . .

IS THAT ALL YOU GUYS **TALK** ABOUT? **DRAGONS**?!

HEY THERE, PHONEY BONE! EIGHT MORE BEERS! WE GOT A LOT OF THIRSTY **CUSTOMERS** TONIGHT!

HEE! HEE! HEE! THIS **DRAGONSLAYER** THING IS **GREAT** FOR BUSINESS!

I GOTTA HAND IT TO YA, PHONEY! I THOUGHT LUCIUS **REALLY** HAD YOU **BEAT** WHEN HE MADE THAT BET TO SEE WHO COULD SELL TH' **MOST BEER!**

I KNOW!! HE'S REALLY **STEAMIN'**, TOO, ISN'T HE?

HE DIDN'T COUNT ON HIS CUSTOMERS' **FEAR OF DRAGONS!**

SPEAKING OF WHICH, O MIGHTY **DRAGONSLAYER,** HOW **ARE** YOU GONNA KEEP YOUR PROMISE TO **SLAY** TH' DRAGONS?

-- HEY, HEY! KEEP YER VOICE DOWN!

I'M NOT GONNA **SLAY** THE DRAGONS! ARE YOU **NUTS?!**

YOU'RE **NOT?!** **BY ST. GEO!** EVERYBODY **HERE** THINKS YOU'RE GONNA GET **RID** OF 'EM!

I WON'T **HAVE TO,** YOU SIMPLETON! THE DRAGONS AREN'T **DANGEROUS!** ONLY TH' **TOWNSFOLK** THINK THEY ARE!

NOW HEADS UP! WE GOT A **CUSTOMER!**

JONATHAN! NOT YOU, **TOO?!** -- YOU WORK FOR **ME!** YOU'RE NOT GONNA TAKE YOUR BUSINESS TO **THEIR** END OF TH' BAR?

it's dragon slay time! Phoney Bone

OH, WELL, **GEE**, MR. DOWN . . . EVERYBODY **ELSE** IS, SO I JUST FIGURED --

DON'T YOU GET IT? ALL THIS TALK ABOUT **DRAGONS** IS JUST A **TRICK** TO GET YOU TO ORDER YOUR DRINKS FROM **HIM**!

HEY, JONATHAN! HOW WAS YOUR CROP LAST YEAR? GOOD HARVEST?

KINDA POOR. WASN'T MUCH RAIN.

YOU KNOW, SOME FOLKS CLAIM IT'S **DRAGONS** THAT CAUSE **DROUGHT**.

THEY **DO**?!! OOH! BUT Y'KNOW? THAT MAKES **SENSE** WHEN YA THINK ABOUT IT!

HOW ABOUT THAT BEER?

MM? OH! YEAH! RIGHT!

FILL 'ER UP!

MY PLEASURE, FRIEND!

I HOPE THIS IS IMPORTANT, LUCIUS! I'M PRETTY **BUSY** OUT THERE!

I DON'T LIKE WHAT YOU'RE DOIN'.

YOU DON'T LIKE WHAT I'M - - ? **WHAT?!** WHAT ARE YOU TALKIN' ABOUT?

I DON'T LIKE WHAT YER DOIN' WITH ALL THIS **DRAGON** STUFF! TH' BET'S OFF!

OFF?! NOW I **KNOW** YOU'RE CRAZY! THIS BET IS TH' BEST THING THAT EVER **HAPPENED** TO THIS JOINT!

JUST LOOK AT TH' PANTRY! DID YOU **EVER** SEE TH' LARDER OVERFLOWIN' LIKE **THAT?** I DID THAT IN **TWO DAYS** WITH ALL THIS **DRAGON** STUFF!

YOU ALMOST STARTED A **RIOT** TH' FIRST NIGHT! YOU THINK RILIN' UP A **MOB** IS WORTH IT JUST TO WIN A LOUSY **BET?!**

FORGET TH' BET -- WE CAN'T **QUIT NOW!** LOOK AT ALL THIS STUFF! WE'RE GETTIN' **RICH!** DON'T FORGET, **HALF** THIS LOOT IS **YOURS!**

I DON'T WANT IT. IT AIN'T **HONEST!**

WHAT'S TH' BIG **DEAL?** EVENTUALLY TH' TOWNSFOLK'LL **REALIZE** THE DRAGONS AREN'T A **THREAT,** AND EVERYTHING WILL GO BACK TO NORMAL -- WHAT'S THE **HARM?**

WHAT'S THE **HARM?** YOU DON'T KNOW WHAT YOU'RE **MESSIN'** WITH, BONE!

OH, YEAH? AN' YOU **DO?**

I KNOW THAT **ONE** DRAGON IN PARTICULAR HAS SAVED YOU AN' YER COUSINS' **BUTTS** MORE THAN A FEW TIMES!

AN' I KNOW TH' DRAGONS DON'T **WANT** ANYBODY TO KNOW THEY EXIST!

NOT THAT **YOU'D** HAVE TH' **DECENCY** TO RESPECT SOMEONE ELSE'S **WISHES!**

Y'KNOW . . .

TH' **IRONY** OF ALL THIS MAY BE LOST ON **YOU** . . .

. . . BUT DON'T YOU THINK IT'S STRANGE THAT **I'M** TH' ONE TELLIN' FOLKS THAT DRAGONS EXIST, AN' **YOU'RE** TH' ONE TRYIN' TO CONVINCE 'EM THAT THEY **DON'T?**

SO?

I'M TH' ONE TELLING 'EM THE **TRUTH!** YOU'RE TH' ONE TRYIN' TO **HIDE** IT! **THAT'S** WHY THEY KEEP COMIN' TO **MY** END OF TH' BAR - - - -

SAY! THAT'S WHAT'S **REALLY** BOTHERIN' YOU, ISN'T IT? THAT I'M WINNING TH' **BET!**

OH, FER . . .

OKAY, PAL, I'M **CALLIN' YOUR BLUFF!** IF YOU WANNA CALL OFF THIS BET, ALL YOU GOTTA DO IS WALK OUT THERE AN' TELL EVERYBODY TH' **TRUTH!**

GO AHEAD! TELL 'EM DRAGONS ARE **REAL!**

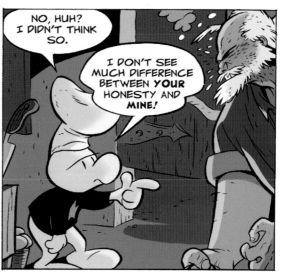

NO, HUH? I DIDN'T THINK SO.

I DON'T SEE MUCH DIFFERENCE BETWEEN **YOUR** HONESTY AND **MINE!**

I GOT A BUSINESS TO RUN.

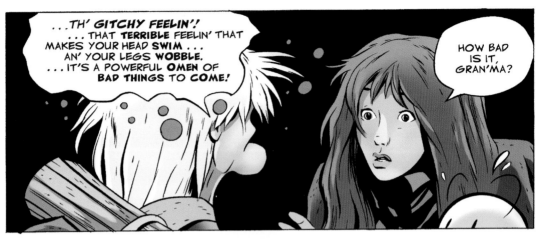

THAT'S INTERESTING . . .

THE MONSTERS DON'T LIKE YOU TOUCHING MY WEAPON.

YOU MAY BE CLOSER TO THE **TURNING** THAN I REALIZED.

THE **TURNING**?

WAIT.

LISTEN!

NOW WHAT?

I DON'T HEAR ANYTHING.

I DON'T EITHER.

THAT'S **GOOD**, RIGHT?

NO, THAT'S BAD. THESE WOODS ARE **FULL** OF RAT CREATURES, AN' AFTER ALL TH' **RUCKUS** WE JUST MADE, THIS PLACE SHOULD BE **CRAWLIN'** WITH 'EM!

MAYBE MORE RAT CREATURES ARE **COMING!**

I DON'T THINK SO...

SOMETHIN'S NOT RIGHT, AND I DON'T **LIKE** IT.

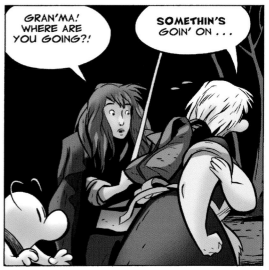

GRAN'MA! WHERE ARE YOU GOING?!

SOMETHIN'S GOIN' ON...

...AN' **THESE** TWO ARE GONNA TELL ME WHAT IT **IS!**

OH, NO YOU DON'T! C'MERE, YOU!

SQUEEE

WHAT'S WRONG, CUZ?

BUSINESS IS **SLOWIN' DOWN!** NOBODY'S BUYIN' OUR **RED DRAGON ALE!**

MAYBE THEY'VE HAD ENOUGH TO DRINK.

PFFFT!

YEAH, RIGHT.

MAYBE YOU NEED A NEW SLOGAN!

WHAT COULD BE BETTER THAN **IT'S DRAGONSLAYIN' TIME?**

HOW ABOUT: **PUT A DRAGON IN YER FLAGON?**

LOOK AT 'EM! THEY'RE **DELIBERATELY** NURSING THOSE BEERS! I WONDER IF **LUCIUS** IS UP TO SOMETHING. . .

MAYBE EVERYBODY SPENT ALL THEIR EGGS.

THAT'S NOT IT. WE ACCEPT **GOODS** AND **LIVESTOCK,** TOO! NO, THERE MUST BE SOME **OTHER** REASON THEY'RE HOLDING OUT.

THEY'RE **PROBABLY** SAVIN' ALL THE **GOOD** STUFF FOR THE BIG SUMMER **PICNIC!**

PICNIC? WHAT PICNIC? I DIDN'T HEAR ABOUT A **PICNIC!**

YOU **HAVEN'T?** I HEARD ABOUT IT FROM **LUCIUS!** EVERY MIDSUMMER'S DAY THERE'S A **HUGE PICNIC** AN' EVERYBODY **BRINGS** STUFF!

I **KNEW IT!** I KNEW THAT BIG APE WOULD FIND **SOME** WAY TO INTERFERE WITH MY PLANS!

DON'T WORRY, I'M SURE YOU'RE **INVITED!**

HE'S DIVERTING MY **FUNDS!** AND **THESE** BACKSTABBERS - -

RRRRR RRRRR!

HOLDIN' OUT ON **ME,** AFTER I OFFERED TO **SAVE** THEIR **CRUDDY LITTLE TOWN** FROM **DRAGONS!**

OOH!

OOH!

YOU FLAT-LANDERS **DISGUST** ME.

CRUNCH CRUNCH

HOW YOUR INFERIOR RACE HAS MANAGED TO **RULE** THIS VALLEY FOR SO LONG IS BEYOND ME.

BUT THIS GAME IS **OVER.**

FAREWELL, YOUR **MAJESTY** - -

URK-

EARTH . . . .

. . . AND **SKY** . . .

HUH HUH HUH

IT'S OVER, DEAR. WE WON'T SEE ANY MORE RAT CREATURES FOR A LONG WHILE.

HOW -- HOW DO YOU KNOW?

IT'S THEIR WAY. I'VE SEEN IT BEFORE.

THORN!

THORN! GRAN'MA! ARE YOU OKAY?!

YES! YES! OH, THANK GOODNESS!

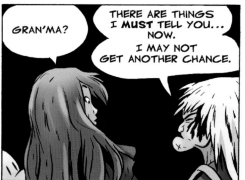

BUT YOU WERE HIDDEN AS A CHILD BECAUSE YOU ARE A **VENI-YAN-CARI**. AN **AWAKENED ONE!** AND YOU HAVE A **TERRIBLE** PATH BEFORE YOU.

GRAN'MA?

AN AWAKENED ONE CAN WALK FREELY BETWEEN THE **WAKING WORLD** AND THE **DREAMING WORLD!** AGENTS OF THE **LOCUST** WILL BE SEARCHING FOR YOU.

WHOA! GRAN'MA! WHAT ARE YOU **TALKING** ABOUT?

THEY'LL HAVE TO GO THROUGH **ME** FIRST!

hmm.

I DON'T THINK THEY'LL EVEN NOTICE YOU, BONE . . . AGENTS OF THE LOCUST WILL STOP AT **NOTHING** TO FREE THEIR MASTER.

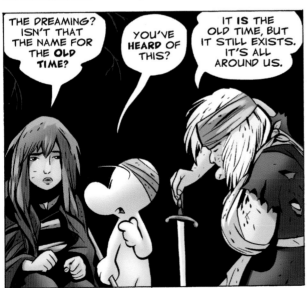

THE DREAMING? ISN'T THAT THE NAME FOR THE **OLD TIME**?

YOU'VE **HEARD OF** THIS?

IT **IS** THE OLD TIME, BUT IT STILL EXISTS. IT'S ALL AROUND US.

IT'S A FORGOTTEN **HUM** THAT ALL THE ANIMALS AND ALL THE TREES ARE STILL LISTENING TO. IT'S JUST **US** WHO CAN'T HEAR IT ANYMORE.

MOST OF US, ANYWAY.

THERE ARE THOSE WHO ARE **TRAINED** TO LISTEN . . .

THERE ARE REPORTS COMING OUT OF THE EASTERN MOUNTAINS THAT THE **RAT CREATURES** HAVE A NEW **LEADER**. A LEADER WHO WEARS A **HOOD** PULLED DOWN OVER HIS **FACE** . . .

THIS IS IN KEEPING WITH THE TRADITIONAL MANNER OF THE DISCIPLES OF **VENU**, WHO, IN THE DAYS OF **OLD**, WERE THE GUARDIANS OF THE KINGDOM.

THE DISCIPLES OF VENU ARE ALSO A MYSTICAL **SECT.** A RELIGIOUS ORDER DEVOTED TO THE STUDY OF **DREAMS** . . .

MY FEAR IS THAT THIS **ROGUE** DISCIPLE LEADING THE RAT CREATURES MAY BE PLANNING A FORBIDDEN **RITUAL** . . .

A RITUAL INTENDED TO **FREE** THE LOCUST USING EITHER MY GRANDDAUGHTER, OR YOUR COUSIN **PHONCIBLE.**

THAT'S WHY WE'RE TAKING THORN TO THE ANCIENT CITY OF ATHEIA, WHERE SHE'LL BE **SAFE.**

I'M NOT GOING TO ATHEIA.

I'M NOT GOING **ANYWHERE** WITH **YOU.** YOU'RE **CRAZY!**

DEAR, YOU'RE **UPSET** -- LISTEN TO ME -

LISTEN TO YOU? **WHY?** EVERYTHING YOU EVER **TOLD** ME WAS A **LIE!**

NO, DEAR! **LISTEN!** WHAT I'M TELLING YOU IS **TRUE!**

THIS IS SUDDENLY THE **TRUTH?!** MY PARENTS ARE DEAD, AND I'M A **PRINCESS** WITH **MAGIC POWERS?!!**

WHAT DOES THAT MAKE ME?!

A **FAIRY** PRINCESS?

THANK YOU **SO MUCH.**

SORRY.

IT **IS** TRUE! ON THE DAY YOU WERE BORN, THE DRAGONS CAME TO US . . .

THEY TOLD US THEY COULD SEE YOUR DREAMS ON THE HORIZON LIKE A **PILLAR OF FIRE.**

LET GO!

HEY, THORN! WAIT UP!

ARE YOU OKAY?

MM... I DON'T KNOW.

I'M SORRY ABOUT THAT **FAIRY PRINCESS** REMARK. I DON'T KNOW WHAT I WAS **THINKING** -- IT JUST POPPED OUT!

IT'S ALL RIGHT.

IT **WAS** KINDA FUNNY.

THE MEN OF PAWA HAVE **TURNED** AND JOINED YOUR ARMY . . . THE ANCIENT CITY OF THE EAST IS ONCE AGAIN **YOURS,** MY LORD . . . .

WHAT OF THE KINGDOM OF ATHEIA?

A CONTINGENCY OF TROOPS IS MASSING ALONG THE BORDER THAT RUNS BETWEEN **PAWA** AND **ATHEIA** . . . THEY AWAIT YOUR INSTRUCTIONS . . .

THERE WILL BE A GREAT BATTLE THE LIKES OF WHICH ATHEIA HAS **NEVER** SEEN . . . .

ENOUGH.

WHAT ARE YOU DOING TO FREE US?

THE ONE WHO BEARS A STAR REMAINS IN THE SMALL NORTHERN VILLAGE OF **BARRELHAVEN** . . .

THE GIRL. WHERE IS THE GIRL?

SHE IS ALSO IN THE VILLAGE . . . ALL OUR ENEMIES ARE THERE . . . . THE **QUEEN MOTHER,** THE **PRINCESS,** THE **BONES** . . . . . . AND THE **GREAT RED DRAGON** . . .

ONCE THE FINAL CAMPAIGN **BEGINS** . . . WE WILL **CRUSH** THIS VILLAGE . . . AND DESTROY YOUR ENEMIES IN **ONE SWIFT BLOW!**

YES, WE DID WELL WHEN WE CHOSE YOU.

THANK YOU, LORD.

YOU ARE OUR EYES AND OUR EARS, MY LOVE. ANSWER ME THIS QUESTION . . .

YES, MY LORD?

WHAT WAS THE FLASH WE SAW ON THE EDGE OF THE DREAMING?

KINGDOK WAS BADLY WOUNDED IN AN ENCOUNTER WITH THE PRINCESS . . . A DOORWAY TO THE DREAMING WAS TEMPORARILY OPENED.

SHE IS TURNING.

PERHAPS.

ANOTHER ATTEMPT MUST BE MADE TO REACH HER.

IF THE ATTEMPT FAILS?

IF SHE CANNOT BE OURS . . . . SHE MUST BE DESTROYED . . . GO NOW.

DO NOT FAIL.

YOU HESITATE . . .

WHAT DO YOU NEED . . . . THE **GIRL** FOR?

SHE IS STRONG.

. . . BUT HER POWER MAY BE USED **AGAINST** US . . . . WOULD IT NOT BE SAFER TO JUST **DESTROY** HER - -

BRING HER TO US.

BUT YOU HAVE **ME** . . . . . . I . . . . . . AM YOUR EYES . . .

I . . . . . . AM YOUR EARS . . .

HAVE NO FEAR . . .

WE HAVE NOT FORGOTTEN . . . YOUR SERVICE TO US . . .

HERE, MR. PHONEY BONE, IT'S A BOTTLE OF OUR **BEST** WINE! ME AN' TH' MISSUS JUST WANTED YOU TO **HAVE** IT.

MM? OH, YEAH, GREAT. THANKS.

WHAT'S TAKING **FONE BONE** AND **THORN** SO LONG? DON'T THEY KNOW IT'LL BE **DARK** SOON?

THEY WERE PROBABLY EATEN BY THE **SAME** DRAGON THAT ATTACKED THEM **LAST** NIGHT!

WE **TRIED** TO KEEP THEM FROM GOING BACK OUT. SHOULD WE START POSTING THE **NIGHT SENTRIES**?

HOLD ON. **HEY, JONATHAN!** ANY SIGN OF TH' SEARCH PARTY?

NOPE. NOT SINCE THEY WENT OUT THIS **MORNING!**

AN' **LUCIUS** ISN'T BACK YET, EITHER? WE'RE GONNA HAFTA PUT UP TH' **GATES** SOON.

HEY! HERE **COMES** SOMEBODY!

IT'S **THEM!**

DID YOU FIND GRAN'MA BEN?

NOTHING. NOT A **TRACE** OF GRAN'MA BEN **OR** LUCIUS!

BUT **YOU'LL** BE JOINING US, RIGHT, FONE BONE?

I WOULDN'T **MISS** IT.

WE'LL BE WAITING IN THE **BIG ROOM** OVER TH' **BAR!**

ARE YOU OKAY, THORN?

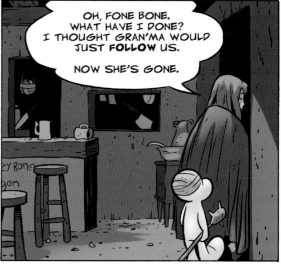

OH, FONE BONE. WHAT HAVE I DONE? I THOUGHT GRAN'MA WOULD JUST **FOLLOW** US.

NOW SHE'S GONE.

DON'T WORRY. WE'LL FIND HER.

NICE ROOM.

IT DOESN'T MATTER TO ME. ALL I WANT TO DO IS **SLEEP**!

OKAY, THEN. SEE YOU IN TH' MORNING.

PLEASANT DREAMS.

I'LL DO MY BEST.

COME IN! COME IN!

WHOA.

WHO DIED AN' MADE **YOU** KING?

NOT **BAD,** EH, CUZ?

WHAT ARE YOU UP TO? WHAT'S WITH THAT **STOCKADE** YOU HAD PUT UP AROUND TH' **SQUARE?** AN' WHY ARE TH' TOWNSPEOPLE PUTTIN' YOU UP IN SUCH **HIGH STYLE?**

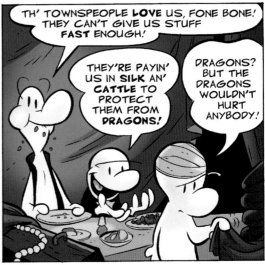

TH' TOWNSPEOPLE **LOVE** US, FONE BONE! THEY CAN'T GIVE US STUFF **FAST** ENOUGH!

THEY'RE PAYIN' US IN **SILK** AN' **CATTLE** TO PROTECT THEM FROM **DRAGONS!**

DRAGONS? BUT THE DRAGONS WOULDN'T HURT ANYBODY!

THAT'S THE **BEST PART!**

YA GOTTA **ADMIT** - - IT SURE MAKES **OUR** JOB EASY!

YOU GUYS **KILL** ME! DON'T YOU HAVE TH' SLIGHTEST **QUALMS** ABOUT **PROFITING** OFF OF OTHER PEOPLE'S **FEARS** AN' **PARANOIA?**

NO, WE DON'T HAVE ANY **QUALMS.** WE'RE JUST GIVIN' 'EM WHAT THEY **WANT!** IF THEY WANNA BE **VICTIMS,** LET 'EM!

YOU CAN'T FEEL SAFE UNLESS THERE'S SOMETHIN' TO BE SAFE AGAINST!

EXACTLY! PEOPLE LIKE TO BE VICTIMS! THERE'S A CERTAIN UNASSAILABLE MORAL SUPERIORITY ABOUT IT . . .

BESIDES, AS LONG AS THEIR GUARD IS UP, I'LL BE SAFE FROM TH' RAT CREATURES!

HMM.

AH, QUIT GETTIN' YER KNICKERS UP IN A BIND. WE'RE NOT GONNA BE HERE MUCH LONGER, ANYWAY!

I'M WORKIN' ON A SCHEME RIGHT NOW THAT'S GONNA PAY OFF BIG! GET US OUTTA DEBT, AND OUTTA THIS VALLEY SCOT-FREE -- AND I SHOULD HAVE ENOUGH PLUNDER LEFT OVER SO WE CAN LIVE LIKE KINGS WHEN WE GET BACK TO BONEVILLE!

COUNT ME OUT.

I'M NOT GOIN' BACK.

I'M STAYIN' HERE!

YOU'RE WHAT?

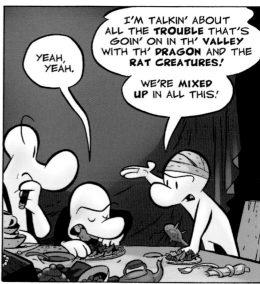

THE STRAGGLER

SEZ YOU!

OH, YEAH? THEN WHY ARE THE RAT CREATURES LOOKING FOR YOU? AN' WHY IS TH' RED DRAGON APPEARING IN MY DREAMS?

I DON'T KNOW, AN' I DON'T CARE! AFTER MIDSUMMER'S DAY, I'M OUTTA HERE WHETHER YOU COME OR NOT!

THAT'S GREAT, PHONEY. JUST GREAT. YOU DO THAT.

THAT'S WHAT YOU ALWAYS DO, ISN'T IT? TAKE CARE OF YOURSELF FIRST!

YOU'LL NEVER CHANGE!

FONE BONE!

DON'T WORRY. HE'LL BE BACK.

SLAM!

WHAT ABOUT OUR MIDSUMMER'S DAY PLAN? HOW WILL WE GET HOME WITHOUT HIS HELP?

HMMM.... I THINK WE'RE GONNA HAVE TO FIND SOME OTHER WAY TO GET A DRAGON ...

BOSS.

HMMF!

PHONEY'S UP TO **SOMETHING** - - AN' WHEN IT **BACKFIRES**, HE'S GONNA EXPECT ME TO GET HIM OFF TH' HOOK - - **AGAIN!**

CRASH BUMP

RUSTLE! RUSTLE!

WHOOP.

THERE'S SOMETHING **MOVIN'** AROUND IN TH' **TRASH** PILE!

RUSTLE **BUMP!** CRUNCH

JEEZ. I WONDER WHAT **THAT** WAS? PROBABLY JUST SOME LITTLE ANIMAL LOOKING FOR FOOD.

CRASH!

WH-WHO'S **THERE?**

SSSSS!

AAAAH!

FONE BONE?
OH, THANK
GOODNESS!

WERE YOU HAVING
ONE OF THOSE WEIRD
DREAMS? 'CAUSE, **MAN**,
IT WAS **REALLY** HARD
TO WAKE YOU UP!

I'M A LITTLE
DIZZY --

WHY'D YOU WAKE
ME UP?

UM,

WE HAVE A
LITTLE
PROBLEM . . .

WHAT
IS IT?

YOU KNOW HOW
TH' **RAT CREATURES**
EVACUATED THE
VALLEY?

SSS.

OH,
MY --

WELL, I THINK
THEY MIGHT'VE
LEFT SOMEBODY
BEHIND.

SSSS.

GET THAT THING
OUT OF HERE!

THORN!
IT'S JUST A **CUB!**
IT'S **HARMLESS!**
HE'S EVEN
FRIENDLY!

THOSE THINGS KILLED MY
PARENTS!! HOW COULD
YOU BRING ONE INTO
MY ROOM?!!

WHOA!
LISTEN --
I'M
SORRY!

WHAT DO YA **MEAN** YOU GOT **ORDERS** TO LET ME IN?

WE GOTTA GET **PERMISSION** FROM TH' **BOSS** BEFORE WE LET ANYONE PASS TH' **GATE!**

DID YOU FIND **GRAN'MA BEN?**

NO, I'M SORRY, JONATHAN, I DIDN'T FIND HER.

WHILE YOU WERE OUT LOOKIN' FOR GRAN'MA BEN, **WE** WERE BUSY PUTTIN' UP THESE **GATES!**

YEAH! THANKS TO TH' NEW **BOSS,** WE'RE FINALLY **DOIN'** SOMETHIN' TO PROTECT OURSELVES FROM **DRAGONS!**

IS THAT RIGHT? AND JUST **EXACTLY** WHO **IS** THIS NEW **BOSS** -- AS IF I DIDN'T KNOW?

HE IS!

PSST!

HEY, SMILEY!

GOOD MORNIN', FONE BONE!

YOU GOT A MINUTE? I NEED YOUR HELP WITH SOMETHING!

SURE, CUZ! WHAT'S UP?

C'MERE! IT'S BACK IN THE STABLES!

LUCIUS! YA BIG LUG! WELCOME BACK!

WHAT DO YOU THINK OF OUR SECURITY FENCE? PRETTY GOOD FOR SUCH SHORT NOTICE, DON'T YOU THINK?

I UNDERSTAND I NEEDED YOUR PERMISSION TO GET BACK INTO TOWN.

JUST A PRECAUTION, FRIEND. YOU CAN'T BE TOO CAREFUL THESE DAYS - - WE WANT TO KEEP THE INSIDERS IN, AND THE OUTSIDERS OUT!

I SEE. AND THIS IS A DECISION YOU'VE MADE IN YOUR CAPACITY AS BOSS?

I'M DOING THIS OUT OF CONCERN, THAT'S ALL. THE WORLD IS A VERY DANGEROUS PLACE, AND WE WANT TO KEEP IT AT A DISTANCE!

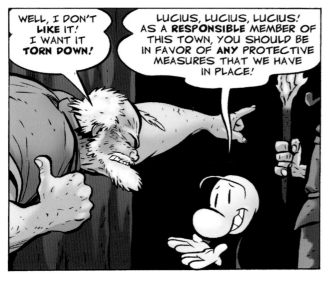

WELL, I DON'T LIKE IT! I WANT IT TORN DOWN!

LUCIUS, LUCIUS, LUCIUS! AS A RESPONSIBLE MEMBER OF THIS TOWN, YOU SHOULD BE IN FAVOR OF ANY PROTECTIVE MEASURES THAT WE HAVE IN PLACE!

WHY, YOU--

YOU DO CARE ABOUT THE SAFETY OF YOUR NEIGHBORS, DON'T YOU?

WHY, YOU **RUNT!** THERE'S NEVER BEEN A **DRAGON** IN THIS TOWN! WE DON'T NEED **YOU** TO PROTECT US!

ARE YOU DONE?

YOU'RE NOT FOOLIN' **ANYONE,** PHONEY BONE! YOU PLANNED THIS WHOLE **DRAGONSLAYER** THING JUST TO PUT YOURSELF IN **CHARGE!**

ARE YOU **DONE?**

IF YOU THINK I'M GONNA CHECK WITH **YOU** EVERY TIME I WANNA GO **IN** OR **OUT,** YOU'RE **CRAZY!**

ARE YOU DONE? **GOOD.** BECAUSE I CAN'T SEE **WHY** YOU WOULDN'T WANT TO **COOPERATE** WITH SOMETHING THAT GUARANTEES TH' **SAFETY** OF YOUR NEIGHBORS.

NOW, WE'D LIKE TO OFFER YOU SOME SHELTER FOR THE NIGHT . . . BUT **UNFORTUNATELY** WE'RE USING YOUR ROOM AT TH' TAVERN FOR OUR **COMMAND CENTER.**

SO! WE FIXED UP A LITTLE PLACE FOR YOU TO SLEEP IN THE **KITCHEN!**

WHA--?! YOU TOOK OVER MY BAR?! WHY, I'M GONNA--

HOLD IT, LUCIUS!

WE'RE WITH TH' **BONE** ON THIS! WE **WANT** HIM TO PROTECT US!

SINCE WHEN DO YOU GUYS LISTEN TO ANYTHING **PHONEY** SAYS?

SINCE HE STARTED TELLIN' US TH' **TRUTH** ABOUT **DRAGONS!**

WENDELL . . .

I'M SORRY, LUCIUS, BUT WE GOT FAMILIES TO THINK ABOUT. YOU FALL IN LINE, OR YOU GET OUT.

IS THAT TH' WAY **ALL** YOU BOYS FEEL?

EUCLID?

RORY?

JONATHAN?

WELL, WELL, WELL.

NOW THAT **THAT'S** SETTLED, I THINK YOU'LL FIND THE ACCOMMODATIONS IN TH' KITCHEN TO BE SUITABLY **SPARTAN** . . .

FORGET IT!

I'LL SLEEP IN TH' **BARN!**

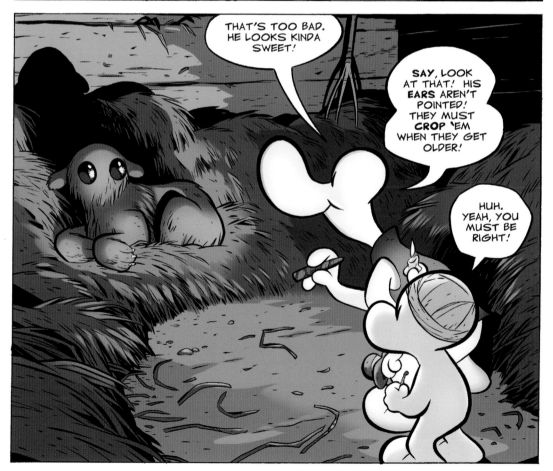

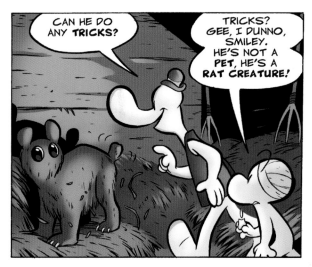

WHO'S IN THERE?

CREEEEK

SPEAK UP! WHO'S THERE?

IT'S US, MR. DOWN! FONE BONE AND SMILEY BONE!

FONE BONE! WHERE'S ROSE? WHERE'S THORN? HAS ANYTHING HAPPENED TO THEM?

THORN IS SAFE -- SHE'S SLEEPING AT THE TAVERN! I DON'T KNOW WHERE GRAN'MA IS!

WHEN DID YOU SEE HER LAST? WAS SHE ALL RIGHT?

YES! YES! SHE AND THORN HAD A FIGHT! THORN RAN OFF, AN' GRAN'MA WANTED ME TO FOLLOW HER! WHEN I LEFT GRAN'MA BEN, SHE WAS STANDING OUT IN THE WOODS!

BUT BEFORE I WENT SHE HANDED ME THIS!

YOU GOT THIS FROM GRAN'MA BEN?

YES. SHE WANTED ME TO TELL YOU THAT THE RAT CREATURES HAVE EVACUATED TH' VALLEY!

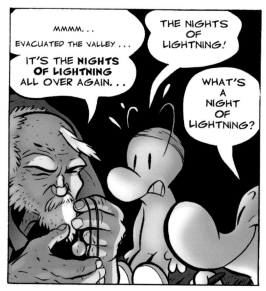

MMMM...
EVACUATED THE VALLEY...
IT'S THE **NIGHTS OF LIGHTNING** ALL OVER AGAIN...

THE NIGHTS OF LIGHTNING!

WHAT'S A NIGHT OF LIGHTNING?

IT'S A **VICIOUS ATTACK** BY THE **RAT CREATURES!!**

ROSE MUST THINK THE RAT CREATURES ARE GOING TO BREAK TH' **TREATY.**

GULP!

WILL THEY COME HERE?

THIS IS TH' TREATY ZONE.

DID ROSE TELL YOU ANYTHING ELSE? DID SHE SAY WHERE SHE WAS GOING?

NO...

BUT SHE **DID** TELL US THE TRUTH ABOUT HER BEING THE **QUEEN OF ATHEIA,** AN' THAT **THORN** IS THE **HEIR TO THE THRONE!**

HEL-LO!

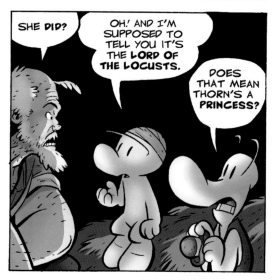

SHE **DID?**

OH! AND I'M SUPPOSED TO TELL YOU IT'S THE **LORD OF THE LOCUSTS.**

DOES THAT MEAN THORN'S A **PRINCESS?**

THAT'S ODD. THE LORD OF THE LOCUSTS WAS AN ANCIENT ENEMY OF THE **DRAGONS!** I THOUGHT HE GOT TURNED INTO **STONE** OR SOMETHING BACK WHEN THE **DRAGONS** STILL RULED THE EARTH.

GRAN'MA WAS PRETTY **UPSET** ABOUT IT - -

SACRÉ BLEU!

WHAT **ELSE** DID ROSE TELL YOU?

WE TALKED ABOUT THORN'S **DREAMS**. AND . . . THORN CAN HEAR SOME KIND OF **HUM** THAT THE REST OF US **CAN'T** HEAR . . .

HEY!

ROSE TOLD YOU **QUITE A BIT**, DIDN'T SHE?

WE HAD A FEW ROUGH DAYS, YEAH.

OH! SHE ALSO TOLD US ABOUT THE **DISCIPLES OF VENU** -- THESE **MONKS** WHO STUDY DREAMS AND WEAR THEIR HOODS PULLED DOWN OVER THEIR **FACES!**

THE **STICK-EATERS**. THEY'RE A MILITARY ORDER THAT WENT UNDERGROUND WHEN THE KINGDOM FELL.

THE DREAMING! THAT'S WHAT GRAN'MA KEPT CALLING IT. I GUESS THESE STICK-EATERS STUDY DREAMS.

HEY!

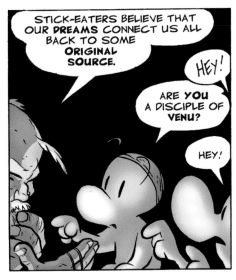

STICK-EATERS BELIEVE THAT OUR **DREAMS** CONNECT US ALL BACK TO SOME **ORIGINAL SOURCE**.

HEY!

ARE **YOU** A DISCIPLE OF **VENU?**

HEY!

DO I LOOK LIKE A HOLY MAN TO YOU?

HEY! IS THORN A **REAL** PRINCESS WITH A **CROWN** AN' EVERYTHING?

HOW DO **I** KNOW, SMILEY? YEAH, WITH A CROWN AN' EVERYTHING! TH' WHOLE WORKS!

WHAT **HAPPENED** THE OTHER NIGHT, BONE? WE HEARD YOU YELLIN' ABOUT A **DRAGON**, BUT BY THE TIME WE **GOT** THERE, ALL WE FOUND WAS **BLOOD** SPATTERED ON THE GROUND.

I WAS CALLING OUT TO TH' DRAGON FOR **HELP**, BECAUSE WE WERE BEING ATTACKED BY A **GIANT RAT CREATURE CALLED KINGDOK!**

I **KNOW** THAT MONSTER.

I THINK KINGDOK HAD IT OUT FOR GRAN'MA BEN, BUT THORN WAS ABLE TO RESCUE HER . . .

SHE **CUT OFF** KINGDOK'S ARM WITH GRAN'MA'S **SWORD!**

WHAM!
JUST LIKE THAT!!

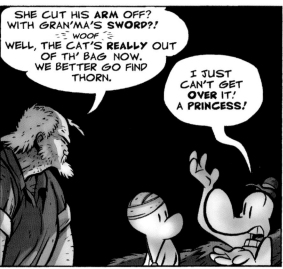

SHE CUT HIS **ARM** OFF? WITH GRAN'MA'S **SWORD?!**
WOOF
WELL, THE CAT'S **REALLY** OUT OF TH' BAG NOW. WE BETTER GO FIND THORN.

I JUST CAN'T GET **OVER** IT! A **PRINCESS!**

I MEAN, **WHO'D** HAVE THOUGHT THAT OUR LITTLE THORN - - LIVING IN A **COTTAGE** WITH HER **GRANDMOTHER** OUT IN THE MIDDLE OF AN **OLD, DARK FOREST** - - WOULD TURN OUT TO BE A **PRINCESS?!**

UNBELIEVABLE!

THINK SHE'LL LET ME WEAR THE **CROWN?** I BET I'D LOOK **COOL** WITH A CROWN . . .

Y'KNOW . . . LUCIUS WAS RIGHT ABOUT **ONE** THING . . .

YEAH? WHAT'S THAT?

THERE'S NEVER BEEN A DRAGON IN THIS TOWN.

SO?

JUST GOT ME **THINKIN'**, THAT'S ALL.

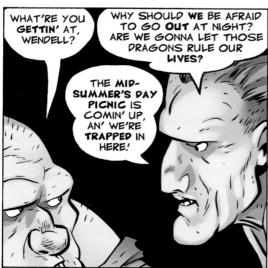

...FAR TOO LONG HAVE WE BEEN FORCED TO LIVE ON THE BARREN SLOPES OF THE **HIGH PLACES** ...

MEN OF **PAWA**, WHO COME FROM THE STURDY HILLS OF THE SOUTH .... NO LONGER WILL YOUR FAMILIES TOIL IN THE DUST AND ROCKS OF YOUR FARAWAY LAND ...

HAIRY MEN OF THE MOUNTAIN TRIBES! YOUR WEARY YEARS OF OPPRESSION AND HUMILIATION ARE NEAR THEIR END ...

OUR DAY HAS COME ...

FOR THE LORD OF OUR DREAMS AND THE KING OF ALL MISTS SPEAKS TO YOU THROUGH ME ... AND DELIVERS US THESE **LAWS** ...

LAWS WHICH ARE PROCLAIMED FOR **ALL** TO HEAR -- SO SPEAKS THE LORD OF THE LOCUSTS --

LAW THE FIRST: ALL THE VALLEYS AND ALL THE LANDS BETWEEN THE MOUNTAINS OF THE RISING SUN, AND THE MOUNTAINS OF THE SETTING SUN, BELONG NOW AND FOREVER TO THE PEOPLE OF THE HOLY HOUSE OF **MISTS**. -- SO SAYETH THE LORD OF THE LOCUSTS --

COULD BE TODAY, TOMORROW AT TH' LATEST.

WHAT ABOUT THE **BLACKSMITH?** IF WE'RE GONNA DEFEND THIS TOWN AGAINST **DRAGONS**, WE NEED TO START BEATING THOSE PLOWSHARES INTO **SWORDS**, YOU KNOW!

EUCLID'S GOT SOME OF TH' BOYS HELPIN' HIM MOVE THE **FORGE** THIS AFTERNOON.

VERY **GOOD**, WENDELL! LOOKS LIKE EVERYBODY'S UNDER MY **CONTROL** –

I MEAN, IT LOOKS LIKE YOU HAVE **EVERYTHING UNDER CONTROL!**

YES, SIR.

SAY, **WENDELL**, HAVE YOU SEEN **SMILEY** BONE? HE TOOK OFF AFTER **BREAKFAST**, AN' HE NEVER SHOWED UP FOR **LUNCH** ...

YOUR COUSIN **MISSED** A MEAL? THAT **IS** STRANGE!

SPEAKING OF MEALS, WENDELL, I NOTICED THAT MY **OMELET** THIS MORNING WAS A LITTLE **SMALLER** THAN USUAL. AND AT **LUNCH**, THE SERVING OF HAM WAS A BIT **STINGY**...

THE VILLAGERS AREN'T **HOLDIN' OUT** ON ME, ARE THEY? A **DRAGONSLAYER** HAS TO KEEP UP HIS **STRENGTH!** I COULD BE CALLED UPON TO FIGHT A DRAGON **AT ANY MOMENT!**

ACTUALLY, SIR, THE **BOYS** WANTED ME TO TALK TO YOU ABOUT THAT.

OH, REALLY.

THE **BOYS** ARE WORRIED ABOUT MY **HEALTH?**

NO, SIR. NOT EXACTLY.

I SHOULD **WARN** YOU, WENDELL, THAT **MOOD** CAN AFFECT A DRAGONSLAYER'S READINESS, **TOO!**

THE MIDSUMMER'S DAY PLAN

IT'S JUST THAT TH' BOYS THOUGHT THAT A LOT OF **TIME** AN' **EFFORT** COULD BE SAVED IF YOU ACTUALLY WENT OUT AND **SLAYED** A **DRAGON!**

SO **THAT'S** HOW IT'S GONNA BE, HUH? **HOLDIN' OUT ON ME, HUH?!**

NO, IT'S JUST THAT WE'VE BEEN **FEEDIN'** YOU AN' YOUR COUSINS FOR OVER A **WEEK**, AN' YOU HAVEN'T GONE OUT TO KILL DRAGONS EVEN **ONCE!**

DON'T GET **CHEAP** ON ME, WENDELL! IF YOU CAN'T AFFORD TO HAVE A **DRAGONSLAYER** AROUND, JUST **SAY** SO, BUT DON'T GO **HOLDIN' OUT** ON ME!

WE'RE **NOT** HOLDIN' OUT ON YOU! WE **PAID** YOU TO BE A **DRAGONSLAYER**, AN' WE WANT YOU TO **SLAY** A **DRAGON!!**

FOR **SHAME!** YOU THINK I DON'T **KNOW** YER **HOLDIN' OUT ON ME?** YOU THINK I DON'T **KNOW** ABOUT THE **MIDSUMMER'S DAY PICNIC?**

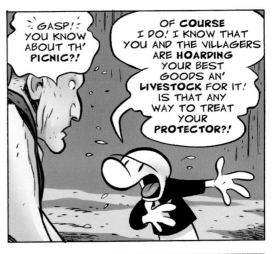

GASP! YOU KNOW ABOUT TH' **PICNIC?!**

OF **COURSE** I DO! I KNOW THAT YOU AND THE VILLAGERS ARE **HOARDING** YOUR BEST GOODS AN' **LIVESTOCK** FOR IT! IS THAT ANY WAY TO TREAT YOUR **PROTECTOR?!**

B-BUT THE PICNIC IS A **TRADITION!** IT MEANS SO MUCH TO THE **CHILDREN!**

HOARDER!

THIS IS A STATE OF **EMERGENCY**, MISTER! WE DON'T HAVE TIME FOR **FRIVOLOUS** CELEBRATIONS!

NOW, YOU AN' THE **BOYS** GATHER UP ALL THESE **GOODIES** YOU BEEN HIDIN' FROM ME, AND BRING 'EM TO TH' CENTER OF TH' COMPOUND AT **DUSK** . . .

. . . AND BRING TH' **VILLAGERS!** IT'S TIME YOU ALL LEARNED ABOUT MY PLANS FOR **MIDSUMMER'S DAY!**

THAT WENDELL'S A LOUSY **INGRATE** JUST LIKE TH' **REST** OF 'EM! I'LL SHOW 'EM THEY CAN'T HOLD OUT ON **PHONCIBLE P. BONE!**

I WONDER WHERE **SMILEY BONE** IS? HE'S **NEVER** AROUND WHEN I WANT HIM!

MOST OF MY **MIDSUMMER'S DAY** PLAN IS READY, BUT THERE ARE STILL A FEW THINGS THAT NEED TO BE TAKEN CARE OF.

OH, WELL, I GUESS AN **ENTERPRISING, YOUNG DRAGONSLAYER'S** WORK IS **NEVER DONE!**

GOOD AFTERNOON, LUCIUS, OL' PAL!

WHAT DO **YOU** WANT?

TAX COLLECTION! TH' DEFENSE OF THIS TOWN AIN'T **FREE,** YA KNOW! EVERYBODY'S GOTTA **CHIP IN!**

GET LOST.

HEY, WE GOT A **DOZEN** DISPLACED **FAMILIES** LIVING IN TH' COMPOUND! WE GOTTA FEED 'EM **SOMEHOW!**

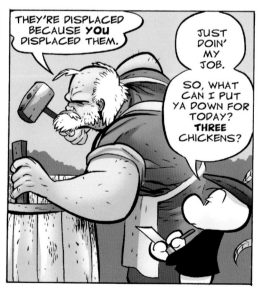

THEY'RE DISPLACED BECAUSE **YOU** DISPLACED THEM.

JUST DOIN' MY JOB. SO, WHAT CAN I PUT YA DOWN FOR TODAY? **THREE** CHICKENS?

THE MIDSUMMER'S DAY PLAN

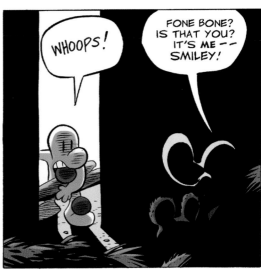

WHOOPS!

FONE BONE? IS THAT YOU? IT'S ME -- SMILEY!

SMILEY BONE? WHAT ARE **YOU** DOING HERE?

I'VE BEEN HERE ALL DAY SMUGGLIN' IN **FOOD** FOR TH' BABY **RAT CREATURE!**

OH! WELL, I GUESS I DIDN'T NEED TO BRING ALL **THIS,** THEN.

DON'T WORRY, IT WON'T GO TO WASTE --

SAY, YOU DIDN'T HAPPEN TO BRING ANY **SALT,** DIDJA?

SNIFF SNIFF

CREEK

FONE BONE?

I KNOW YOU'RE IN HERE . . .

UM . . . YEAH, I'M IN HERE, THORN . . .

I ALSO KNOW THIS IS WHERE YOU'RE KEEPING THAT **RAT CUB.**

WHA--!

CUB?

I --

DON'T WORRY. I WON'T HURT IT.

IN FACT, I'VE COME TO APOLOGIZE FOR MY BEHAVIOR LATELY. MAY I SIT DOWN?

OH, SURE. PULL UP SOME HAY.

THANK YOU. I DON'T REALLY KNOW HOW TO BEGIN . . .

THORN, YOU DON'T HAVE TO - -

THE DREAMS ARE GETTING WORSE.

WHAT? THEY ARE?

YES. THEY'RE **SO** BAD THAT I'M AFRAID TO GO TO SLEEP.

I HAD NO IDEA - - ARE YOU OKAY?

I CAN'T TELL. I'M SO TIRED THAT EVEN WHEN I'M **AWAKE** IT FEELS LIKE A DREAM.

THORN, THIS IS **SERIOUS**! WE GOTTA **DO** SOMETHIN'!

WHAT'S **HAPPENING**, FONE BONE? WHY IS EVERYTHING **CHANGING**?! WHY CAN'T WE GO BACK TO THE WAY IT WAS **BEFORE**?

UM . . .

I WANT TO GO HOME.

HOME? WHAT ARE YOU TALKIN' ABOUT?

I'M GOING BACK TO THE FARMHOUSE.

THE FARMHOUSE? **THAT** WON'T HELP ANYTHING! DON'T YOU **REMEMBER**? GRAN'MA BEN SAID IT WASN'T **SAFE** THERE ANYMORE!

I DON'T CARE. I'M GOING BACK.

SAY! LISTEN . . .

. . . WHY DON'T YOU STAY HERE WITH ME AN' **SMILEY**? YOU COULD **HELP** US!

WE'RE GONNA SNEAK TH' **CUB** OUT OF TH' **COMPOUND** TONIGHT, AN' SET HIM **FREE**!

NO.

I HAVE TO GO.

THORN, YOU'RE **TIRED**! YOU'RE NOT MAKING A **RATIONAL** DECISION!

THINK ABOUT IT . . . JUST PROMISE ME YOU'LL **THINK** ABOUT IT BEFORE YOU LEAVE . . .

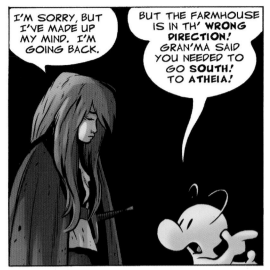

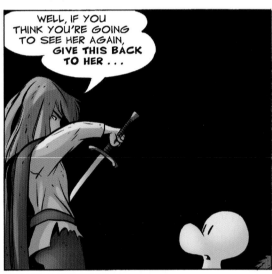

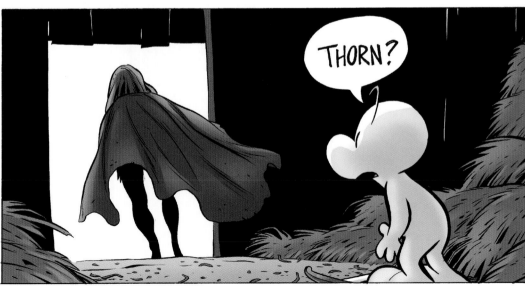

WHAT'S ALL TH' EXCITEMENT ABOUT, BIG GUY?

YOUR PARTNER IN CRIME IS ABOUT TO MAKE A **SPEECH!**

PHONEY BONE? WHAT'S **HE** UP TO?

FRIENDS! FRIENDS! THANK YOU FOR COMING!

I WISH WE COULD HAVE GATHERED UNDER HAPPIER **CIRCUMSTANCES** . . .

BUT IT HAS COME TO MY ATTENTION THAT THE **TREMENDOUS** PILE OF **WEALTH** THAT I'M STANDING ON WAS **SECRETLY** STOCKPILED AWAY FOR THE **MIDSUMMER'S DAY PICNIC!**

TSK! TSK!

I'M **VERY** DISAPPOINTED.

NOT **ONLY** WERE YOU HIDING IT FROM ME . . . WHICH IS BAD **ENOUGH** . . . BUT **LOOK** WHAT YOU'VE DONE TO **YOURSELVES!**

ALL THIS **HOARDING!** ALL THIS **DECEIT!**

THIS IS THE SORT OF THING THAT **ATTRACTS** DRAGONS AND OTHER HOUSEHOLD PESTS IN THE **FIRST** PLACE!

PEOPLE! PEOPLE! DON'T YOU **SEE?!** YOU **BROUGHT** THIS PLAGUE OF DRAGONS ON **YOURSELVES** WITH **ILLICIT BEHAVIOR!**

OH, FER TH' LOVE OF . . .

WE MUST **ROOT OUT** THIS MORAL DECAY IN OUR MIDST BEFORE IT'S **TOO LATE!**

GO TO YOUR HOMES AND GET EVERY SINGLE THING OF VALUE THAT YOU OWN, AND **BRING IT HERE IMMEDIATELY!**

... ONLY **THEN** CAN THE HEALING PROCESS BEGIN ...

THAT'S IT, STEP ASIDE!

THIS VILLAGE HAS A PROBLEM WITH ITS **MORAL FIBER!**

OH, IT HAS A PROBLEM WITH **MORALS,** ALL RIGHT...

YOUR MORALS ARE STARTIN' TO GET IN MY **FACE!**

DRAGONS ARE A **COWARDLY** AND **GREEDY** SPECIES! THEY LOVE PEOPLE WHO **HOARD** THINGS!

YOU'RE GOING TOO FAR THIS TIME, PHONEY BONE!

I AM THIS VILLAGE'S **SWORN** DRAGONSLAYER! EVERYTHING I **DO,** I DO TO **PROTECT** THE PEOPLE OF BARREL-HAVEN!

PROTECT US? HOW?! WITH THAT LITTLE **FENCE** YOU MADE OUT OF **TWIGS?!** THAT FENCE WOULDN'T STOP A RAT CREATURE, LET ALONE A DRAGON!!

WHAT DO YOU CARE, ANYWAY? ACCORDING TO **YOU,** DRAGONS DON'T EVEN **EXIST!**

THEY EXIST, ALL RIGHT, AN' YOU DON'T KNOW ANYTHING ABOUT 'EM!

SO! YOU **FINALLY** ADMIT THAT DRAGONS **DO EXIST!** YOU **ADMIT** THAT IT'S ME WHO'S TELLING THE **TRUTH!**

YES, DRAGONS **EXIST!** AND THEY'RE ALL AROUND US! -- BUT THEY'RE NOT LIKE **YOU** SAY THEY ARE! TH' DRAGONS ARE **GOOD!**

YOU'RE MIXIN' EVERYBODY **UP!**

IF THEY'RE SO **GOOD,** WHY DO YOU HAVE TO **LIE** ABOUT THEM?

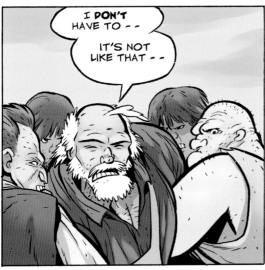

I **DON'T** HAVE TO --

IT'S NOT LIKE THAT --

JUST TELL ME **ONE THING,** LUCIUS -- JUST **ONE** THING -- IF YOU **KNEW** DRAGONS WERE **REAL** ALL ALONG, WHY DID YOU **TELL** EVERYONE THEY WERE **MAKE-BELIEVE?**

HUH? WHY?!

WHAT'S THE MATTER, LUCIUS? **CAT** GOT YER TONGUE?

OR MAYBE THE **REAL** QUESTION IS: DOES A **DRAGON** HAVE YOUR TONGUE?

...HMM. I THOUGHT AS MUCH.

THE DRAGONSLAYER

AS I WAS **SAYING**, DRAGONS ARE A **COWARDLY** SPECIES...

...IF WE CAN MAKE AN EXAMPLE OF **ONE** DRAGON, WE CAN **SCARE OFF** THE REST!

MY PLAN IS SIMPLE! **LURE** ONE INTO A **TRAP!**

TOMORROW IS MIDSUMMER'S EVE! I WANT ALL THIS **BOOTY** -- ALONG WITH ALL TH' **LOOT** UP IN MY ROOMS -- LOADED ONTO **WAGONS!**

I WILL **LEAD** THIS WAGON TRAIN **OUT OF THE VALLEY** AND OVER THE MOUNTAINS TO THE PASS CALLED **THE DRAGON'S STAIR!**

THERE, WE'LL BUILD AN **ALTAR**, AND **USE** THIS TREASURE AS **BAIT!**

AND **WOE** TO THE HAPLESS DRAGON WHO STUMBLES INTO **MY** TRAP, BECAUSE **DRAGON-KEBABS** BEGIN AT SUNRISE!

THIS EMERGENCY MEETING OF THE DRAGONSLAYER HIGH COUNCIL...

...IS ADJOURNED.

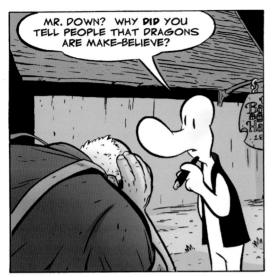

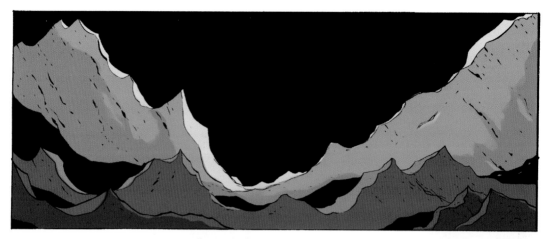

'BUT THE BONES ARE SIMPLE *FOOLS*, AND THE PRINCESS IS JUST A *CHILD*! SURELY, YOU DO NOT NEED *MYSELF* OR MY *BEST WARRIORS* FOR SUCH A MISSION.'

WHY DO YOU *QUESTION* YOUR *ORDERS*? . . . . THAT *CHILD* AND HER FOOLS *CUT OFF YOUR ARM!* THAT SHOULD BE REASON ENOUGH FOR *YOU* . . . . .

REVENGE IS NEVER FAR FROM MY THOUGHTS, O LORD, BUT THE WAR COMES FIRST . . .

DO THEY POSE A *SERIOUS* THREAT TO OUR *CONQUEST* OF THE VALLEY?

KINGDOK, MY WORTHY COMMANDER . . . TAKING LAND AWAY FROM OUR ENEMIES IS NOT ALL THAT THIS WAR IS ABOUT . . .

. . . . NO . . . . IT IS MUCH *MORE* THAN THAT . . . .

FONE BONE, I'VE GOT THE CUB WITH ME . . . WE'RE READY TO GO.

OKAY, SMILEY, OKAY! I JUST WANT TO GIVE THORN A FEW MORE MINUTES. SHE MIGHT SHOW UP.

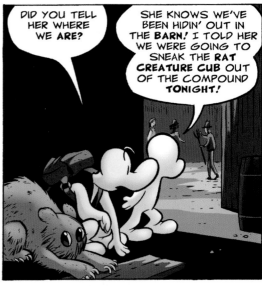

DID YOU TELL HER WHERE WE ARE?

SHE KNOWS WE'VE BEEN HIDIN' OUT IN THE BARN! I TOLD HER WE WERE GOING TO SNEAK THE RAT CREATURE CUB OUT OF THE COMPOUND TONIGHT!

I DON'T THINK SHE'S COMING.

I THINK SHE'S GOIN' BACK TO HER GRAN'MA'S HOUSE.

SIGH.

YOU'RE PROBABLY RIGHT.

I THOUGHT SHE MIGHT CHANGE HER MIND. SHE'S BEEN SO DEPRESSED LATELY, I WAS HOPING THIS MIGHT SNAP HER OUT OF IT. . . GET HER MOVING AGAIN, INSTEAD OF SITTIN' AROUND IN THAT ROOM.

BUT WE CAN'T WAIT FOREVER! IF EVERYTHING'S CLEAR ON YOUR SIDE, WE BETTER GET STARTED!

I DON'T THINK WE'LL HAVE ANY MORE TROUBLE WITH **LUCIUS**, BUT POST A COUPLE OF GUARDS ON THAT PILE OF **TREASURE** JUST TO BE SURE.

YES, **SIR!** BOY, THIS IS **EXCITING!** I CAN'T **WAIT** TO GO OFF AN' SLAY THE **DRAGON** TOMORROW!

IS SOMEBODY GETTIN' THAT **WAGON TRAIN** TOGETHER? WE'RE GONNA NEED THOSE **COWS** FIRST THING IN THE MORNING!

DON'T WORRY, MR. BONE, **WE'LL** BE READY.

GOOD, BECAUSE THE SOONER THAT **TREASURE** IS LOADED UP ON THE COWS, THE SOONER WE HEAD OFF TO DO **MIGHTY BATTLE** WITH THAT **MARAUDING DRAGON!** AND THAT'S WHAT YOU **WANT**, RIGHT?

OH, **YES, SIR!** THE SOONER WE **FIX** THAT DRAGON, THE SOONER WE CAN GET OURSELVES **BACK** ON THE **PATH** OF **RIGHTEOUSNESS!**

VERY GOOD. SAY, JONATHAN, YOU HAVEN'T SEEN MY **COUSINS** AROUND ANYWHERE, HAVE YOU?

NO, SIR, NOT FOR A COUPLE OF **DAYS!**

WELL, SEE IF YOU CAN **FIND** THEM! IT'S IMPORTANT THEY GO **WITH** US TOMORROW!

YOU CAN COUNT ON **ME**, SIR!

RRRR!

WHERE TH' HECK ARE **FONE BONE** AND **SMILEY BONE?** DON'T THEY **KNOW** I'M ABOUT TO PULL OFF THE **GREATEST SCAM** OF MY CAREER **AND** GET US BACK TO **BONEVILLE** AT THE SAME TIME?!!

H'LO THERE, PHONEY BONE!

HEY! **SHOO!**

BEAT IT!

PESKY BUG!

HOLD IT! HOLD IT! IT'S **ME,** TED!

WHO? OH, YEAH.

WHAT DO **YOU** WANT? MAKE IT **QUICK** -- I'M A BUSY MAN.

I HEARD YOU WAS LOOKIN' FOR YOUR **COUSINS!**

WHOA! WHOA! I **AM!** YOU KNOW WHERE THEY ARE?

MAYBE I **DO,** AN' MAYBE I **DON'TS.**

THIS IS NO TIME FOR **GAMES,** BUG! I GOT A **PROBLEM!** I'M LEAVING FOR BONEVILLE **TOMORROW,** AND I GOTTA FIND MY **COUSINS!**

BONEVILLE? I HEARD YOU WAS GOIN' OUT TO SLAY THE **DRAGON!**

I DON'T THINK FONE BONE WOULD BE TOO **HAPPY** ABOUT YOU SLAYIN' HIS BEST FRIEND!

YEAH, YEAH.

YOU'RE **BREAKIN'** MY HEART. JUST TELL ME WHERE MY COUSINS ARE!

NO! NOT AS LONG AS YOU IS PLANNIN' ON **SACRIFICIN'** TH' **DRAGON** --

OH, FOR --

LISTEN, YOU'RE A **FRIEND** OF FONE BONE'S, RIGHT?

YEAH... WHAT ARE YOU **UP** TO, PHONEY BONE?

WHAT IF I TOLD YOU THERE WASN'T GONNA **BE** ANY SACRIFICE? WOULD YOU TELL ME WHERE FONE BONE IS **THEN?**

WHAT'RE YOU TALKIN' ABOUT?

I'M JUST TRYIN' TO GET THE TOWNSFOLK TO **ESCORT** ME OUT OF THE VALLEY WITH A **WAGON TRAIN** FULL OF **TREASURE!** NO ONE'S GONNA GET HURT! **TRUST ME!**

GET OUTTA **TOWN!**

EXACTLY! THE TOWNSFOLK **THINK** WE'RE GOIN' INTO THE MOUNTAINS TOMORROW TO **CATCH A DRAGON**, BUT **REALLY**, MY COUSINS AND I ARE GONNA GIVE 'EM TH' **SLIP** AND RETURN TO **BONEVILLE IN TRIUMPH!**

HOW YOU GONNA GIVE 'EM TH' SLIP? AIN'T THEY GONNA **NOTICE** YOU GOT TH' **TREASURE?**

THAT'S THE **BEST PART!** EVERYBODY **KNOWS** DRAGONS LOVE **TREASURE**, RIGHT? WELL, **THESE** YOKELS THINK WE NEED THE TREASURE FOR **BAIT--** SO WHEN WE GO TO SET THE **TRAP**, WE CAN JUST **SLIP OFF** INTO TH' DARKNESS!

DOES FONE BONE KNOW ABOUT THIS LITTLE SCHEME?

NO! THAT'S THE **PROBLEM!** HE DOESN'T KNOW **ANYTHING** ABOUT IT! IF I CAN'T FIND FONE BONE AND SMILEY **TONIGHT**, THEY'LL **NEVER** GET BACK TO **BONEVILLE!**

WELL... I SEEN 'EM HANGIN' AROUN' THE **BARN** A LOT LATELY. MAYBE YOU SHOULD LOOK **THERE.**

THANKS, BUG!

NOW, REMEMBER! DON'T **TELL** ANYBODY OR YOU'LL RUIN FONE BONE'S CHANCE TO GET HOME!

YOU'S A **THIEF** AN' A **CROOK**, PHONCIBLE P. BONE, AN' ONE DAY IT'S GONNA **CATCH UP** TO YA!

YEAH, YEAH!

FONE BONE? YOU IN HERE?

SMILEY - - ?

HEY, WHAT'S THIS?

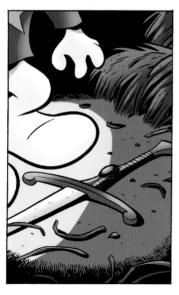

CREAK!

FONE BONE?

IS THAT YOU?

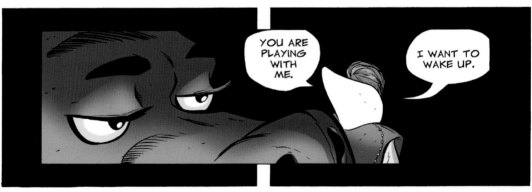

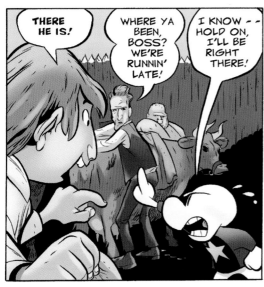

THERE HE IS!

WHERE YA BEEN, BOSS? WE'RE RUNNIN' LATE!

I KNOW -- HOLD ON, I'LL BE RIGHT THERE!

WHAT'S **WRONG**, MR. BONE?

FONE BONE AND SMILEY BONE DIDN'T COME BACK LAST NIGHT! THEIR BEDS WEREN'T EVEN **SLEPT IN!**

THE PEOPLE HAVE SPOKEN! IN CASE YOU DIDN'T **CATCH** THAT, **LUCIUS**, OLD PAL, THEY PICKED **ME!**

- - NOT YOU - -

ME!

I ALREADY SOLD MORE **BEER** THAN YOU, AND ACCORDING TO OUR **AGREEMENT**, IF THE TOWNSFOLK **LIKE** THE WAY **I** RUN THINGS, THEN ALL DEBTS ARE **CANCELED!**

UNLESS, OF COURSE, YOU HAVE ANY **OBJECTIONS?**

DIDN'T THINK SO.

SEE YA AROUND, LUCIUS!

ALL RIGHT, PEOPLE, **MOVE 'EM OUT!!**

Moo!

Moo!

THREE CHEERS FOR THE DRAGONSLAYER!

YAY!

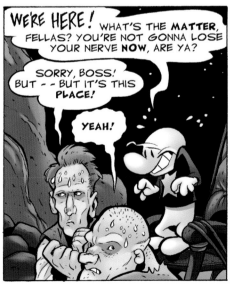

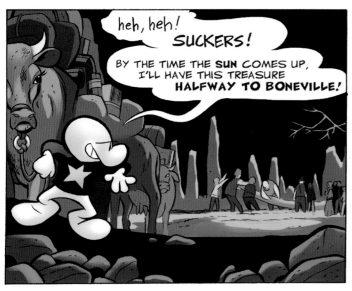

WHAT'S TH' **MATTER**, PHONEY BONE? AIN'TCHA GLAD TA **SEE** ME? IT'S ME, TED!

YOU!

AH, YOU **IS** GLAD!

SAAAY! WHERE'S **FONE BONE** AN' **SMILEY?** YOU'RE NOT SLIPPIN' OFF WITHOUT YER **COUSINS**, ARE YA?

NO, I'M NOT SLIPPIN' OFF WITHOUT MY COUSINS.' **THEY** SLIPPED OFF WITHOUT **ME!**

AIN'TCHA GONNA TRY TO **FIND** 'EM?

LISTEN UP, **BUG!** THEY'RE **GONE!** FOR ALL **I** KNOW, THEY'RE BACK IN BONEVILLE **RIGHT NOW!**

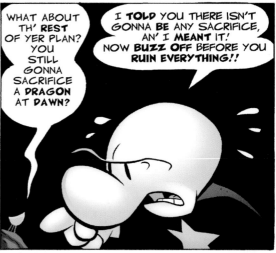

WHAT ABOUT TH' **REST** OF YER PLAN? YOU STILL GONNA SACRIFICE A **DRAGON** AT **DAWN?**

I **TOLD** YOU THERE ISN'T GONNA BE ANY SACRIFICE, AN' I **MEANT** IT! NOW **BUZZ OFF** BEFORE YOU **RUIN EVERYTHING!!**

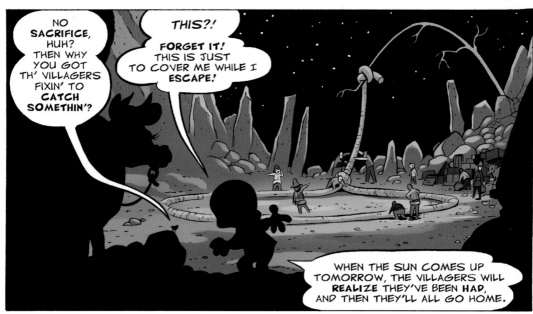

NO SACRIFICE, HUH? THEN WHY YOU GOT TH' VILLAGERS FIXIN' TO **CATCH SOMETHIN'?**

THIS?!

FORGET IT! THIS IS JUST TO COVER ME WHILE I **ESCAPE!**

WHEN THE SUN COMES UP TOMORROW, THE VILLAGERS WILL **REALIZE** THEY'VE BEEN **HAD**, AND THEN THEY'LL ALL GO HOME.

AN' **NOBODY'S** GONNA GET HURT?

TRUST ME! NOTHING IS GOING TO HAPPEN. I'LL SIMPLY FADE INTO THE **NIGHT...** NEVER TO DISTURB YOUR PRECIOUS VALLEY **AGAIN!**

AN' OF COURSE YOU TAKIN' THE TOWNSPEOPLE'S **TREASURE** WITH YOU.

HEY, WHAT CAN I **DO?!** I'M SUPPOSED TO BE LAYIN' OUT TH' **BAIT!** EVERYBODY **KNOWS** DRAGONS CAN'T RESIST **TREASURE!**

SO STEALING THE TREASURE IS JUST A **UNAVOIDABLE** CIRCUMSTANCE.

EXACTLY.

WELL, I WANNA GET YOU OUTTA THE VALLEY AS MUCH AS **ANYBODY,** SO WHAT CAN I DO TO **HELP?**

FIND A GOOD **ESCAPE** ROUTE!

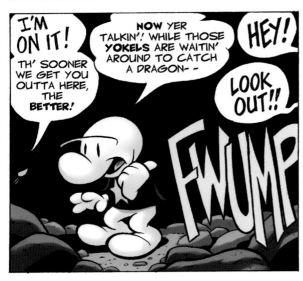

I'M ON IT! TH' SOONER WE GET YOU OUTTA HERE, THE **BETTER!**

NOW YER TALKIN'! WHILE THOSE **YOKELS** ARE WAITIN' AROUND TO CATCH A DRAGON--

HEY!

LOOK OUT!!

FWUMP

WHAT TH --

BOSS!

BOSS!

WE GOT ONE!

WHAT DO WE DO **NOW**?!

JUST STAY CALM! I-- Uh---- I'LL HANDLE IT FROM HERE--

ARE YOU SURE THOSE ROPES WILL HOLD HIM?

THEY WERE MADE TO YOUR SPECIFICATIONS!

GOL'! LOOK AT TH' **SIZE** OF HIM!

GULP!

EVERYBODY! STAY BACK! DON'T BE AFRAID! THE **DRAGONSLAYER** IS HERE!

IT WON'T BE LONG NOW! SOON WE'LL ALL BE BACK ON THE **PATH OF RIGHTEOUSNESS!**

OH, BOY.

DRAGON?

H'LO, PHONEY BONE.

!

HELLO? HELLO?!

WHAT'S **WRONG** WITH YOU?! THAT TRAP WAS OUT IN **PLAIN SIGHT!** **DIDN'T YOU SEE IT?!**

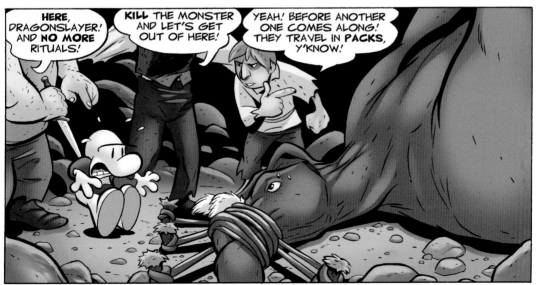

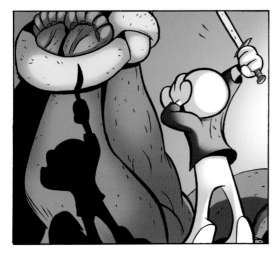

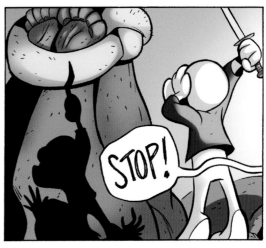

THORN?

WHAT'S SHE DOING THERE?

HEY!

GET THAT **GIRL** OUT OF THERE!

I'M NOT GOING ANYWHERE UNTIL SOMEONE EXPLAINS TO ME WHAT'S GOING ON HERE.

ARE YOU **BLIND?!** LOOK WHAT YOU'RE **STANDING ON!**

MOVE! WE HAVE TO KILL IT BEFORE THE **SUN** IS UP!

PHONCIBLE P. BONE! WHAT HAVE YOU DONE **THIS** TIME?

I--

HE WAS MAKING A DEAL TO SELL US OUT TO THE **ENEMY**!

HE'S A **TRAITOR**!

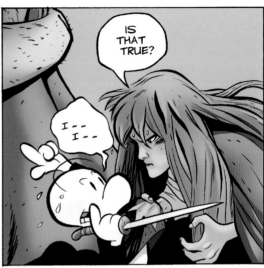

IS THAT TRUE?

I-- I--

WHAT AM I SAYING? OF COURSE IT'S TRUE!

WENDELL! PREPARE YOUR MEN! AFTER WE **FREE** THE DRAGON, WE CAN GO INTO THE VALLEY AND **FACE** THE ENEMY!

FREE THE **DRAGON**?!

THE DRAGON **IS** THE ENEMY!

EEEEEE

FIRE!

FIRE IN THE VALLEY!

IT'S COMING FROM OUR **TOWN**!

IT'S THE **DRAGONS**-- THEY'VE ATTACKED THE **TOWN**!

NO.

IT'S NOT THE DRAGONS . . . IT'S THE **RAT CREATURES**!

WHAT?

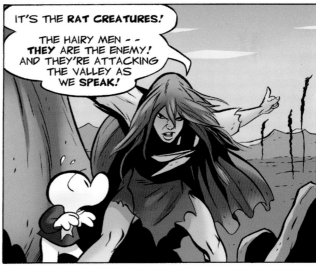

IT'S THE **RAT CREATURES**!

THE HAIRY MEN - - **THEY** ARE THE ENEMY! AND THEY'RE ATTACKING THE VALLEY AS WE **SPEAK**!

DON'T LISTEN TO HER! **KILL THE DRAGON**!

THORN . . . FOR THE GOOD OF THE TOWN- - FOR THE GOOD OF THE **WHOLE VALLEY**- - STAND ASIDE **OR ELSE**!

I WON'T FIGHT YOU, BUT I WILL **NOT** LET YOU HARM THE DRAGON!

TAKE HER DOWN FROM THERE!

WE'RE ALMOST OUT OF TIME!

YES! KILL THE DRAGON **QUICKLY** BEFORE IT'S TOO LATE!

YESSSSS . . . . KILL IT **QUICKLY** . . . .

?

. . . OR WE WILL DO IT **FOR** YOU . . .

AAAH! THE HAIRY MEN!!

. . . THIS WAR IS OVER AND IT HAS SCARCELY **BEGUN** . . .

INSTEAD OF **RESISTING** US . . . YOU HAVE DELIVERED TO US OUR **GREATEST** ENEMY!

...BOUND AND HELPLESS LIKE A LAMB FOR THE SLAUGHTER!

DON'T YOU TOUCH HIM!

SSHNG!

SHING! SHING!

SHING! SHINNG!

? ! GASP!

WH-WHO ARE THEY?

WE'RE TRAPPED!

WHAT--?

DRAGON . . .

THANKS, KID. WE GOT 'EM ON THE RUN.

IF YOU'RE EVER **LOST** -- REMEMBER, THERE ARE **DRAGONS IN THE EARTH.**

NO, WAIT!

DRAGON! **WAIT!** WHERE'S MY GRANDMOTHER? WHERE'S FONE BONE?

WAIT!

PHONEY! WHERE'S FONE BONE?

I DON'T KNOW, THORN! I HAVEN'T SEEN HIM FOR **DAYS!**

This book is for Krishna and Avaday Iyer

ROQUE JA

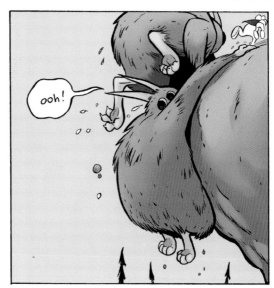

GO ON!!
GET LOST!!!

WE DON'T WANT YOU AROUND HERE!

OKAY! OKAY! THEY'RE GONE!

DID YOU SEE **THAT**, FONE BONE? HE **SAVED** US! YOU **SAVED** US, BARTLEBY! OH, **BOY!** EVERYTHING'S GONNA BE **ACES** FROM NOW ON!

HMM.

WHAT'S THE **MATTER**, CUZ? EVERYTHING'S GONNA BE ACES FROM NOW ON, **RIGHT?** HE **SAVED** US!

WELL . . .

PAT PAT

THE WHOLE REASON WE CAME **UP** HERE WAS TO GIVE BARTLEBY BACK TO THE **RAT CREATURES**, AND LOOK WHAT **HAPPENED!**

YEAH. THAT DIDN'T WORK OUT TOO GOOD, DID IT?

NOW I DON'T KNOW **WHAT** WE'RE DOIN'.

AT THE MOMENT, YOU ARE **TRESPASSING**.

WE, UH... WHO'S THEM?

WHO'S HIM?

COME, COME...

YOU KNOW...

...THEM! THE OLD COW WOMAN AND THE **DRAGONS**.

...OR HIM.

SURELY YOU KNOW OF **HIM** -- THE **MASTER** OF THE **RAT** CREATURES -- **THE HOODED ONE!**

GULP!

THE VALLEY IS DIVIDED IN **TWO**...

EVERYONE **MUST** CHOOSE A SIDE!

WHY?

WE'RE STRANGERS IN THE VALLEY-- ALL WE WANT TO DO IS **RETURN** THIS LOST CUB BACK TO HIS HOME IN THE MOUNTAINS, MISTER-- UH... MISTER--?

I AM **ROQUE JA,** MASTER OF THE EASTERN BORDER. EVERYTHING YOU SEE IN THESE MOUNTAINS BELONGS TO **ME.**

HISS!

ANYTHING THAT **MOVES** IN MY DOMAIN, DOES SO ONLY WITH MY **LEAVE...**

AND THAT **INCLUDES** RAT CREATURES!

OKAY, OKAY, MR. ROCK JAW! WE DON'T WANT TO MESS WITH YOUR **DOMAIN--** WE JUST WANNA TAKE TH' KID **HOME!**

SO, YOU ARE **STRANGERS** IN OUR VALLEY...

YEAH, WE'RE--

..UH..

HOW **INTERESTING.**

FONE BONE! WE DON'T **LIKE** THIS GUY...

BONE, DID YOU SAY?

THE HOODED ONE IS **SEARCHING** FOR SOMEONE NAMED **BONE...**

HE IS?

YES. THE ONE WHO BEARS THE **STAR** IS NAMED **BONE.**

DO YOU **KNOW** HIM, PERHAPS?

A **STAR?** HEY! I THINK HE MEANS **PHONEY BONE!** WHAT'S HE WANT WITH **HIM?**

YEAH! HOLD IT RIGHT THERE, ROCK JAW!

R-R-ROQUE JA! R-R-ROQUE! YOU'RE NOT ROLLING THE **R!**

WHAT'S THIS HOODED GUY WANT WITH OUR COUSIN?

THE VALLEY IS **DIVIDED**, YOU SEE, EVER SINCE THE FALL OF THE KINGDOM, AND THE HOODED ONE SEES IT AS RIPE FOR **PLUCKING.**

BUT HE FEARS THAT A NEW **LEADER** WILL ARISE AND **UNITE THE VALLEY** BEFORE HE CAN **CONQUER** IT.

HOWEVER, IF YOUR COUSIN LOOKS ANYTHING LIKE **YOU TWO**, I HARDLY THINK HE'LL BE A **THREAT!**

ARE YOU TELLIN' ME THAT THE HOODED ONE THINKS **PHONEY BONE** IS GONNA **UNITE THE VALLEY?**

HA!

PHONEY'S NO **LEADER!** HE GOT CHASED OUT OF **BONEVILLE** JUST FOR SAYIN' HE WANTED TO RUN FOR **MAYOR!**

THAT'S ENOUGH, SMILEY. WHO'S SIDE ARE **YOU** ON, ROCK JAW?

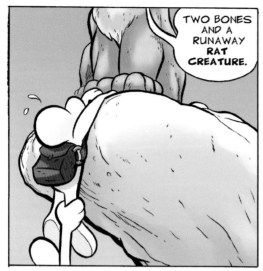

TWO BONES AND A RUNAWAY **RAT CREATURE**.

I IMAGINE THERE WILL BE A SIZABLE **REWARD** FOR BRINGING THE THREE OF YOU IN. . . .

BUT I DON'T WANT ANY MORE **DIFFICULTIES**, SO SEND THE **CUB** UP FIRST.

YOU'RE NOT GONNA SEPARATE **US!**

THE CUB. NOW.

FORGET IT! YOU'LL NEVER GET THIS CUB!

ERF.....

GO ON AN' LEAVE US ALONE! WE DIDN'T DO ANYTHING TO YOU!

I AM WAITING.

SMILEY---
URK

WHA--

BARTLEBY! WHAT ARE YOU - - ?

SIGH.

I'M GLAD **SOMEONE** IS BEING REASONABLE.

COME ALONG.

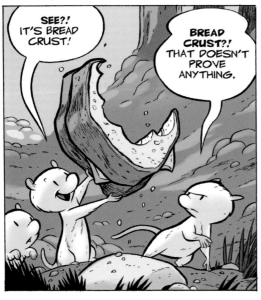

CHAPTER TWO

AND **LOOK** AT THAT!

EEYUH!

ONE OF SMILEY'S **CIGAR STUBS!**

I **TOLD** YOU WE WERE ON THE RIGHT TRAIL!

C'MON! THEY CAN'T BE FAR NOW!

I DUNNO...

WHAT? AREN'T YOU COMIN'?

MM...

WE'RE PRETTY FAR FROM **HOME.** MOM'S GONNA BE **MAD!**

YOU'RE NOT **SCARED,** ARE YOU? **JEEZ!** WE'VE ALREADY COME THIS FAR!

BUT WHAT IF SHE'S **WORRIED** ABOUT US?

WHAT ABOUT **FONE BONE** AND **SMILEY BONE?** WHO'S GONNA WORRY ABOUT **THEM?** THEY DISAPPEARED **DAYS AGO!**

BUT MOM SAID **NEVER** TO GO NEAR TH' **EASTERN MOUNTAINS** 'CAUSE IT MIGHT BE **DANGEROUS --**

SNAP!

WHOOPS. WHAT'S THAT?

LISTEN, YOU! WHAT'S A RACCOON DOING **SNEAKIN' AROUND** IN THE MIDDLE OF THE **DAY**?

I DIDN'T MEAN TO SCARE YOU. ARE YOU OKAY?

WE'RE FINE! WE WERE JUST PLAYIN' **POSSUM**!

YOU DON'T NEED TO BE EMBARRASSED. MY NAME IS RODERICK.

WHY'D YOU SNEAK UP ON US LIKE THAT, **RODERICK**?

I WASN'T SNEAKIN' UP ON **YOU**!

THEN WHAT WERE YOU DOIN' IN TH' **BUSHES**? HIDIN' FROM YOUR **MOMMY**?

YEAH, WHAT WERE YOU DOIN'? HIDIN' FROM YER **MOMMY**?!

I DON'T **HAVE** A MOMMY **OR** A DAD, SO SHUT UP!

OOPS.

OH, MAN. ARE YOU AN **ORPHAN**?

WE'RE SORRY!

WHAT HAPPENED TO YOUR FOLKS?

THEY'RE DEAD! AN' FOR THE LAST TWO DAYS, I BEEN **SPYING** ON THE GUYS WHO DID IT!

?

?

COME WITH ME. I'LL SHOW YOU.

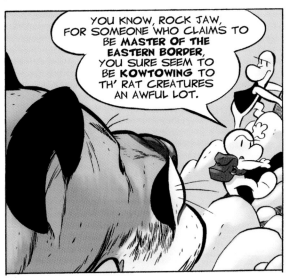

I GUESS THAT DEPENDS ON WHOSE SIDE YOUR **FRIENDS** ARE ON.

WHOSE SIDE?

ROQUE JA SAYS EVERYBODY HAS TO BE ON A SIDE NOW BECAUSE IT'S A **WAR.** YOU CAN EITHER PICK THE **RAT CREATURES** OR THE **DRAGONS.**

I PICK THE **DRAGONS** . . .

. . . I'VE NEVER **SEEN** A **DRAGON,** BUT I KNOW I DON'T LIKE THOSE **RAT CREATURES!**

WELL, WE'RE NOT ON THE RAT CREATURES' SIDE **EITHER!**

BUT WHOSE SIDE IS **HE** ON?

ROQUE JA?

EVERYBODY KNOWS ROQUE JA **HATES DRAGONS** --

UH, OH!

I THINK THE **BONE COUSINS** ARE IN **TROUBLE!**

HIT A **NERVE**, THERE ROCK JAW? WELL, IF YOU THINK WE'RE GOING TO DO **ANYTHING** THAT WILL HELP THE RAT CREATURES, **YOU CAN FORGET IT!**

THAT'S RIGHT! WE'RE **FRIENDS** OF THE VALLEY PEOPLE AN' WE'LL **STOP** YOU!

THE VALLEY PEOPLE . . . **HA!**

THE VALLEY PEOPLE MAY HAVE RULED IN THE **PAST**, BUT THEY LOST CONTROL A LONG TIME AGO.

THIS WAR IS NOW BETWEEN TWO OF THE **ORIGINAL** INHABITANTS OF THE VALLEY:

. . . THE HIGH AND MIGHTY **DRAGONS** . . .

. . . AND THOSE MISERABLE VERMIN **THE RAT CREATURES!**

CREEEK!

I THOUGHT I HEARD SOMETHING . . .

. . . BUT IT MUST HAVE BEEN SOME FALLING ROCKS.

NOW WHAT WAS I SAYING? OH, **YES** . . . THE RAT CREATURES ARE **VERMIN!**

THEY ARE A **POX!**

THEY'RE A **PESTILENCE!** AND EVERY DAY **MORE** OF THEM ARRIVE FROM PAWA AND RUN **AMOK** IN MY BEAUTIFUL MOUNTAINS.

OH, BROTHER. THERE GOES THE NEIGHBORHOOD!

JUST THE **SIGHT** OF THEM ON MY MOUNTAIN **INFURIATES** ME!

C'MON!

I GOT AN IDEA!

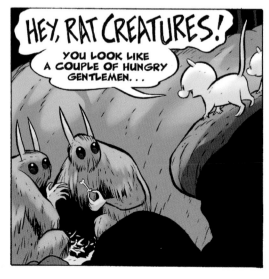

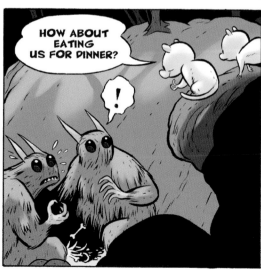

IF YOU DON'T LIKE RAT CREATURES SO MUCH, WHY DON'T YOU TEAM UP WITH THE **DRAGONS** AND CHASE THEM OFF?

BECAUSE THE ONLY THING **WORSE** THAN THE RAT CREATURES ARE THOSE ARROGANT **DRAGONS!**

DO YOU KNOW WHAT THE **VALLEY PEOPLE** THINK ABOUT THE DRAGONS? THEY THINK THE DRAGONS **CREATED THE VALLEY!!**

SO?

SO, THEY THINK THE **QUEEN** OF THE DRAGONS WENT **MAD** ONE DAY, AND ALL THE OTHER DRAGONS WERE FORCED TO COME AND **RESTRAIN** HER . . .

SHE RESISTED, AND OUR LANDSCAPE IS THE RESULT OF THEIR **BATTLE** - - THEY CRASHED AND PUSHED AGAINST THE **MOUNTAINS,** AND CREATED THE **VALLEY.** IN THE END, WHEN THEY COULD NOT **STOP** HER, THEY HAD TO TURN HER TO **STONE!**

IF YOU ASK **ME,** IT'S A FOOLISH **FAIRY TALE** FIT ONLY FOR THE WEAK-MINDED.

DID YOU SAY SHE WAS TURNED TO **STONE?**

HEY!

HERE, KITTY KITTY KITTY!

!

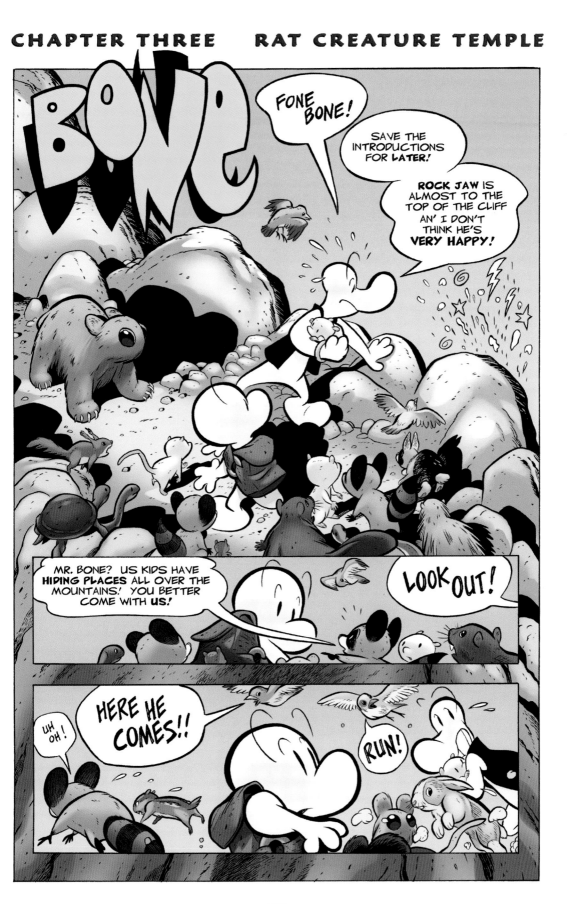

IN HERE, FONE BONE!

PANT PANT

WHEW!

HE CAN'T REACH US! WE'RE **SAFE!**

PEEK OUT AND SEE IF HE'S STILL THERE.

RIGHT!

HE'S STILL THERE.

WHAT ARE WE GONNA DO NOW?

WE MIGHT AS WELL GET COMFORTABLE... THAT GIANT **CAT'S** NOT GOING ANYWHERE! **SCOOT OVER!**

ROCK JAW WILL SIT THERE ALL **DAY!**

HE'LL SIT THERE FOR **TWO** OR **THREE DAYS!** HE'S DONE IT BEFORE!

OHMYGOSH! WE'RE **TRAPPED!**

IS THERE SOME OTHER WAY OUT OF HERE?

YES! THERE'S A **TUNNEL!**

IX-NAY! NOT IN FRONT OF TH' **RAT!**

YEAH! SHUT YER **BEAK!** YOU WANNA GIVE AWAY ALL OUR **SECRETS?**

SORRY!

NOW HOLD ON! **THIS** RAT CREATURE IS WITH **US!** AN' HIS NAME IS **BARTLEBY!**

HE'S JUST A **BABY!**

HE'S STILL A **RAT CREATURE!** AN' RAT CREATURES **EAT** PEOPLE LIKE US!

THEY ATE ALL OUR **PARENTS!**

WELL, **WE** CAME ALL THIS WAY TO RETURN BARTLEBY TO HIS HOME IN TH' MOUNTAINS, AN' WE'RE **NOT** GONNA ABANDON HIM **NOW!**

SMILEY...

IF TH' **BONES** SAY TH' KID IS OKAY, THEN HE'S **OKAY!**

OH, YEAH? AN' WHO ARE **YOU?**

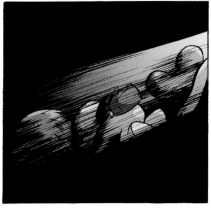

SKRITCH!

WATCH IT. WE'RE IN SOME HUGE OPEN SPACE NOW.

SKRITCH

JUST A LITTLE FARTHER! WE'RE ALMOST THERE!

I HOPE SO. IT'S GETTIN' A LITTLE **STUFFY** IN HERE.

THIS IS IT, SMILEY! THIS IS THE **OPENING!** I'M OUTSIDE!

WHOA.

NOW **THERE'S** SOMETHIN' YOU DON'T SEE EVERY DAY!

YEAH, BOY.

HEY, SMILEY . . .

. . . YOU REMEMBER WHEN WE WERE WITH **ROCK JAW**, HE TOLD US A STORY ABOUT HOW THE VALLEY WAS CREATED?

YEAH, I REMEMBER. A BUNCH OF **DRAGONS** HAD A **FIGHT** AN' PUSHED UP THE MOUNTAINS.

RIGHT! THE QUEEN OF THE DRAGONS WENT MAD AND STARTED ON A **RAMPAGE!** THE **REST** OF THE DRAGONS WERE TRYING TO STOP HER!

AND TH' ONLY WAY THEY COULD **DO** IT WAS TO **TURN HER TO STONE!**

YOU MEAN . . .

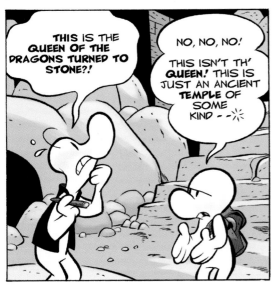

THIS IS THE **QUEEN OF THE DRAGONS** TURNED TO STONE?!

NO, NO, NO! THIS ISN'T TH' **QUEEN!** THIS IS JUST AN ANCIENT **TEMPLE** OF SOME KIND - -

UM. AT LEAST I **THINK** IT'S JUST AN ANCIENT TEMPLE . . .

LISTEN, SMILEY! BEING **TURNED TO STONE** IS THE SAME THING THAT HAPPENED TO **ANOTHER** ANCIENT ENEMY OF THE DRAGONS! THE **SAME** ENEMY WHO IS AFTER **PHONEY BONE** AND **THORN!**

BUT I THOUGHT IT WAS A **FAIRY TALE** AN' NOBODY **BELIEVED** IN DRAGONS ANYMORE!

WE KNOW **SOME** PEOPLE WHO BELIEVE IN THEM -- LIKE **GRAN'MA BEN** AND **LUCIUS DOWN!** I'VE SEEN A DRAGON, **TOO,** REMEMBER?

THE **LORD OF THE LOCUSTS** IS AFTER PHONEY BONE AND THORN, AND HE WAS AN ANCIENT ENEMY OF THE DRAGONS **WHO WAS TURNED TO STONE!**

YOU MEAN TH' **QUEEN OF THE DRAGONS** AND **THE LORD OF THE LOCUSTS** ARE ONE AND THE SAME?

COULD BE. I DON'T KNOW. IT'S A WEIRD COINCIDENCE, ANYWAY.

SO . . . ? IS THIS JUST A TEMPLE OR **NOT?**

PRETTY SURE IT'S JUST A **TEMPLE!** MAYBE IT'S AN OLD **RAT CREATURE** TEMPLE. . .

IN ANY CASE, IT LOOKS **ABANDONED** NOW.

YEAH, YOU'RE RIGHT! IT'S JUST SOME OLD **ABANDONED BUILDING!** BESIDES, EVEN IF IT **WAS** AN OL' ENEMY OF TH' DRAGONS, HOW CAN IT HURT YOU IF IT'S TURNED TO **STONE?**

SAY, WHERE'D THE KIDS GO?

HEY, FONE BONE AND SMILEY BONE! **OVER HERE!**

WE'RE NOT OUT OF DANGER YET! RODERICK SAYS WE WON'T BE SAFE UNTIL WE REACH THE TREE LINE!

ONCE WE'RE IN TH' FOREST **NO ONE** CAN FIND US!

WHAT'S **ROCK JAW** UP TO?

HE'S STILL WATCHING THE UPPER ENTRANCE!

BUT HE'S STARTING TO GET **SUSPICIOUS!**

WE BETTER GET GOING.

IT'S A PRETTY STEEP CLIFF, BUT IT'S THE ONLY WAY DOWN FROM HERE, SO YOU **BIG GUYS** WILL JUST HAVE TO BE **CAREFUL!**

DON'T WORRY ABOUT US! WE CAN HANDLE IT!

LET'S GO!

THIS ISN'T SO STEEP!

WE'RE NOT TO THE **STEEP** PART, YET!

HEY, FONE BONE, HOW YOU COMIN' WITH YER **LOVE POEMS?**

MM?

HEY! HEY! I DON'T WANNA TALK ABOUT **THAT** IN FRONT OF EVERYBODY!

YOU WRITE **LOVE POEMS,** MR. BONE?

C'MON, BONE! TELL US A **LOVE POEM!**

uh...

YES! A LOVE POEM THAT YOU WROTE FOR MISS **THORN!**

WHAT MAKES YOU THINK MY LOVE POEMS ARE FOR **THORN?**

AW, HECK, BONE! EVERYONE **KNOWS** THEY'RE FOR **THORN! JEEZ!**

I'D LIKE TO HEAR A LOVE POEM, MR. BONE!

ME, TOO!

SURE! WE ALL WOULD!

FORGET IT! YOU'LL LAUGH!

COME ON! WE WON'T LAUGH! MAYBE WE CAN HELP **WRITE** ONE!

YES! WE WON'T LAUGH!

WE **PROMISE!**

WE'LL HELP **WRITE** YOUR **LOVE** POEM!

ALL RIGHT, ALL **RIGHT.** LET'S SEE . . .

OKAY, HERE'S ONE THAT ISN'T QUITE FINISHED YET.

AHEM.

IN THE STALLS OF MY **HEART,** DEAR, I'VE BUILT A HORSE-**CART,** DEAR, AND MY DEAR YOU CAN RIDE IT ALL **DAY** . . .

I'VE BUILT IT FROM **LOVE** -- -- FROM THE **CLOUDS** UP ABOVE -- E'EN THE **RAINS** CANNOT WASH IT AWAY!

BUT MY LOVE YOU CAN'T HEAR, SO THE CART WILL NOT **STEER,** AND I'M LEFT WITH A HEART FULL OF HAY.

WOW.

WAIT. I'M NOT DONE --

HA! HA! HA! HA! HA! HA! HA!

LOOK AT BARTLEBY! HE'S COVERING HIS EARS!

EVERYBODY'S A **CRITIC,** HUH, CUZ?

HEY! HE CAN'T EVEN **TALK!**

HA! HA! HA! HA! HA! HA! HAW! HA!

YOU SAID YOU WOULDN'T LAUGH.

I'M **TRYIN'** NOT TO **CRY!**

YEA, BARTLEBY!

HA! HA! HA!

TH' **RAT** ISN'T SO BAD **AFTER ALL!**

HOORAY FOR BARTLEBY! HA! HA!

HMMF!

YOU'RE FROM TH' MOUNTAINS, RODERICK! WHERE'S TH' VILLAGE OF **BARRELHAVEN** FROM HERE?

I'VE NEVER **HEARD** OF BARRELHAVEN BEFORE. SORRY.

WHAT DO YOU THINK, FONE? I MEAN WE **DID** LEAVE **PHONEY BONE** IN THE VILLAGE. YOU DON'T THINK ANYTHING COULD HAVE **HAPPENED** WHILE WE'VE BEEN AWAY?

HMM.

I THINK WE BETTER GET DOWN THERE.

SHOW US WHERE TO GO, KIDS.

WELL, WELL . . . IF IT ISN'T THE BONE COUSINS!

. . . AND THE LITTLE SNOTS WHO PUSHED US **OFF THE CLIFF!**

OH, NO! NOT **AGAIN!**

HEH, HEH, EXCEPT **THIS** TIME, THERE IS NO GIANT **MOUNTAIN LION** AROUND TO INTERFERE!

YESSS! **ROQUE JA** IS STILL KEEPING WATCH ON YOUR LITTLE **MOUSEY HOLE** UP ABOVE!

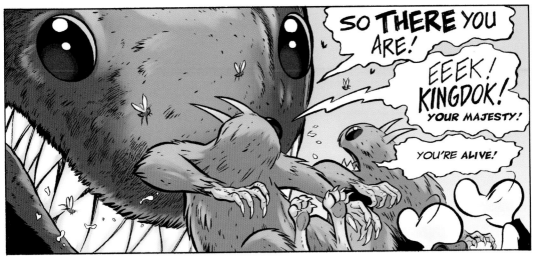

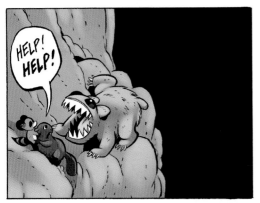

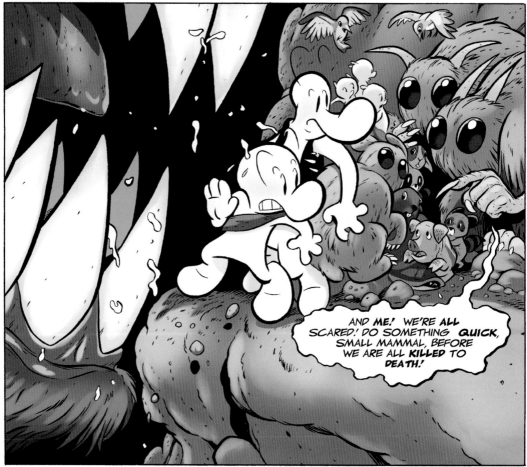

THERE'S **NOTHIN'** THAT WAY EXCEPT FOR **SHEER CLIFF FACE!**

SO?!

WHAT DO **YOU** SUGGEST? DIPLOMATIC NEGOTIATIONS?!

WHY NOT? THE **RAT** CREATURES ARE DESERTERS! LET'S HAND 'EM OVER!

YEAH! KINGDOK SAID THEY WERE **TRAITORS!** MAYBE IF HE HAD **THEM,** HE'D LET US GO!

WAIT, NOW! LET'S TALK THIS OVER!

YEAH!

THROW 'EM TH' RATS!

GRRR!

RRR!

HELP US, SMALL MAMMAL!

SILENCE!

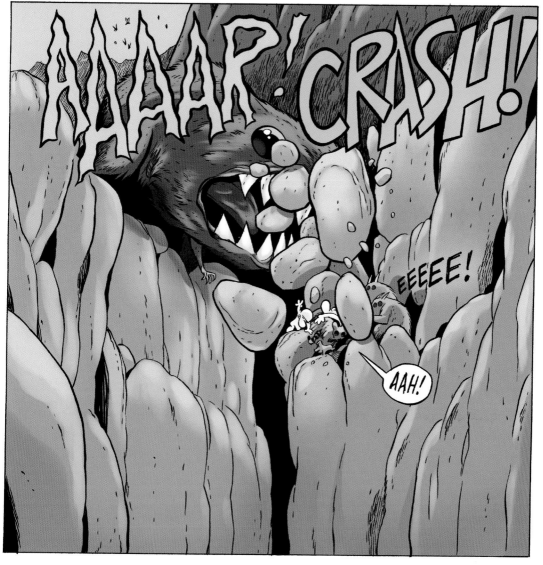

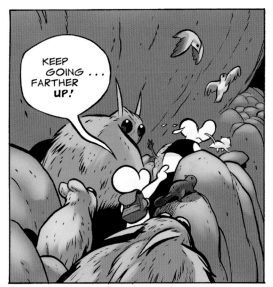

REALLY?

WHY NOT?

BECAUSE YOU **ATE ALL OUR PARENTS!** THAT'S WHY NOT!

SEE? THAT'S WHAT **I** WAS SAYING! WE'RE **NATURAL ENEMIES!** TO **US,** YOU GUYS ALL LOOK LIKE **HORS D'OEUVRES!**

COULD WE DISCUSS THIS FROM A SAFER VANTAGE POINT? LIKE, SAY, A SLIGHTLY LARGER LEDGE?

I DON'T CARE WHAT ANYBODY **LOOKS** LIKE TO YOU FUZZ-FACE, JUST **DON'T** STICK 'EM IN YOUR **MOUTH,** GOT THAT?

YOU'RE NOT TH' BOSS OF ME!

HEY!

IT'S NOT GONNA TAKE KINGDOK LONG TO FIND US, SO HERE'S THE DEAL . . .

UNTIL WE'RE OFF THIS **LEDGE,** WE CALL A **TRUCE!** THAT MEANS WE ALL WORK **TOGETHER!**

IT **ALSO** MEANS **NOBODY EATS ANYBODY!** NO MATTER **WHAT** THEY LOOK LIKE!

HE'S TALKIN' TO YOU!

WATCH IT, BREAD-STICK!

WE AGREE TO YOUR TERMS, SMALL MAMMAL! **NOW GET US OUT OF HERE!**

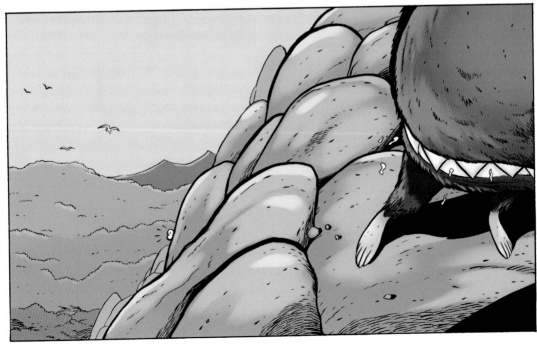

WE'RE DOOMED!

HE'S JUST WAITING FOR US!

ALL RIGHT, ALL RIGHT! WE'RE NOT DOOMED YET! LET'S JUST THINK THIS THROUGH!

SOMEHOW WE HAVE TO GET TO THE SAFETY OF THE **TREES** DOWN THERE ... BUT WE CAN'T GO STRAIGHT DOWN -- IT'S TOO **STEEP!**

AND WE CAN'T GO **BACK**, BECAUSE KINGDOK DESTROYED THE LEDGE!

UP IS OUT, BECAUSE THAT'S WHERE KINGDOK IS **NOW!**

YOU CALL **THIS** THINKING IT THROUGH?

WHATEVER YOU CALL IT, IT LEAVES ONLY **ONE** WAY OUT! **FORWARD!**

BUT-- BUT WE DON'T KNOW WHERE TH' LEDGE **GOES!**

YES! WHAT IF IT TAKES US RIGHT TO **KINGDOK?**

OR BACK TO **ROCK JAW,** THE GIANT MOUNTAIN LION! DON'T FORGET ABOUT **HIM!**

WHAT CHOICE DO WE HAVE?

HOLD ON--

HEY, BIRD KIDS! CAN YOU SEE WHERE THIS LEDGE GOES?

THE LEDGE GETS **SMALLER** AND **SMALLER!**

BUT FARTHER AHEAD IS A **BOULDER FLOW!** IF YOU CAN REACH IT, YOU MIGHT BE ABLE TO WORK YOUR WAY DOWN TO THE TREES!

THIS IS INSANE!

IT'S STUPID!

HEY! NOTHING WE'VE DONE SO FAR HAS BEEN **UN-STUPID,** AND WE'RE STILL **ALIVE,** AREN'T WE?!

I CAN'T REALLY **ARGUE** WITH THAT, BUT I FEEL LIKE I **SHOULD.**

CARRY ON, FONE BONE! MAKE A **STUPID DECISION!**

RIGHT! FOLLOW ME!

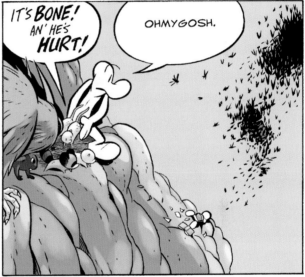

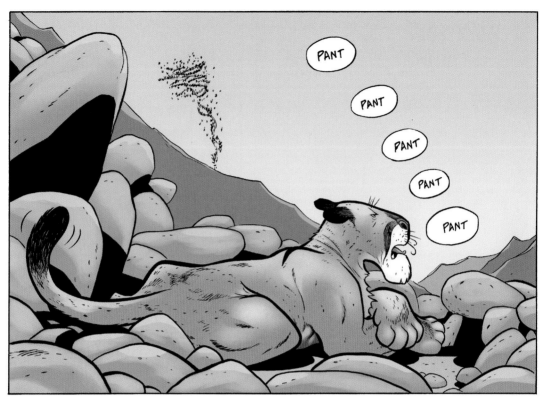

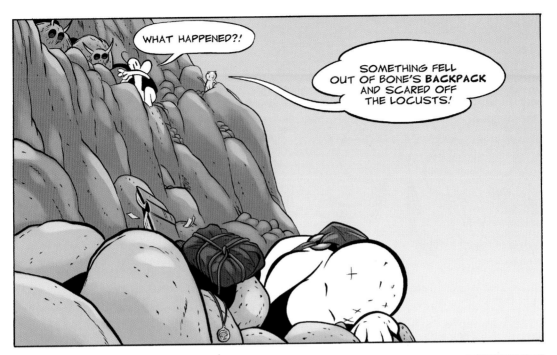

WHAT HAPPENED?!

SOMETHING FELL OUT OF BONE'S **BACKPACK** AND SCARED OFF THE LOCUSTS!

WHERE'S **KINGDOK**?

HE DISAPPEARED!

Poof! VANISHED INTO **THIN AIR!**

UUHN!

IS HE OKAY?

OW OOW. **MAN!** I FELL ON THE **EXACT** SAME SPOT THAT JUST **HEALED!**

HEY! WHAT HAPPENED TO THE **LOCUSTS?**

SOMETHING IN YOUR BACKPACK SCARED THEM OFF! ARE YOU **OKAY?**

WHOA! CHECK IT OUT!

IT LOOKS LIKE A **CROWN!**

OOH!

A **CROWN!** I BET IT BELONGS TO **THORN!**

WHAT'RE YOU DOING WITH **THAT** IN YOUR **BACKPACK,** CUZ?

OH, MY **GOSH!** YOU THINK KINGDOK WAS PART OF A **DREAM?!**

OH, YEAH, FOR **SURE!** SOMETIMES WHEN YOU GO THROUGH THE TEMPLE YOU GET **NIGHTMARES!**

WHOA, WHOA. ARE YOU SAYING KINGDOK **WASN'T** EVEN THERE?! WE JUST DREAMED IT?

YEAH! SEE? **THAT'S HUM-HUM!**

NOW JUST **HOLD ON** -- WHAT ABOUT ALL TH' **ROCKS** THAT WERE CRASHING DOWN **AROUND** US? THE **LEDGE** CRUMBLING OUT FROM UNDER OUR **FEET?**

THINGS GET **CRAZY** AROUND THAT OLD TEMPLE! FOLKS SAY IT WAS BUILT ON A GHOST CIRCLE!

I BET IF WE WENT **BACK,** THE LEDGE WOULD BE **IN ONE PIECE!**

OH, COME **ON!** WE SAW IT -- WE **FELT** IT!

YOU CAN FEEL STUFF WHEN YOU **DREAM!**

!

MAN! WHAT DID YOU SAY THIS TEMPLE WAS BUILT ON?

A GHOST CIRCLE! THAT'S WHERE THE LOCUSTS COME FROM.

VERY DANGEROUS! IF YOU STEP INTO ONE YOU'LL **DISAPPEAR!**

YOU GUYS ARE **SERIOUS!**

COOL!

SMILEY, THE GUY WHO'S AFTER **PHONEY BONE** - - - - HE'S CALLED THE LORD OF THE **LOCUSTS**!

RIGHT, RIGHT! HE PROBABLY CONTROLS THE **LOCUSTS**! HENCE TH' NAME!

I STILL DON'T UNDERSTAND HOW HE COULD INDUCE A **MASS HALLUCINATION** LIKE THAT.

MAYBE WE SHOULD GO BACK AND MAKE SURE PHONEY'S **OKAY**.

THIS GUY IS AFTER **THORN**, TOO! SHE DOESN'T HAVE ANY **IDEA** WHAT SHE'S UP AGAINST!

SHE'S COMPLETELY **VULNERABLE**!

I'LL SAY! THE LOCUSTS COULD MAKE HER BELIEVE **ANYTHING**! **HECK**! THEY COULD MAKE THE WHOLE **VALLEY** BELIEVE ANYTHING!

THAT'S IT! GRAB YOUR **STUFF**! WE HAVE TO GET BACK AND **WARN OUR FRIENDS**!

AYE, AYE, CAP'N!

YOU HEARD TH' **MAN**! LET'S **ROLL**!

YOU THERE! OPEN UP YOUR **MOUTH**!

WHY?

CHECKING FOR SMALL MAMMALS. ANYBODY IN THERE?

HELLO?

HELLO? HELLO?

OKAY, YER CLEAN!

C'MON, SMILEY! GET IT IN GEAR!

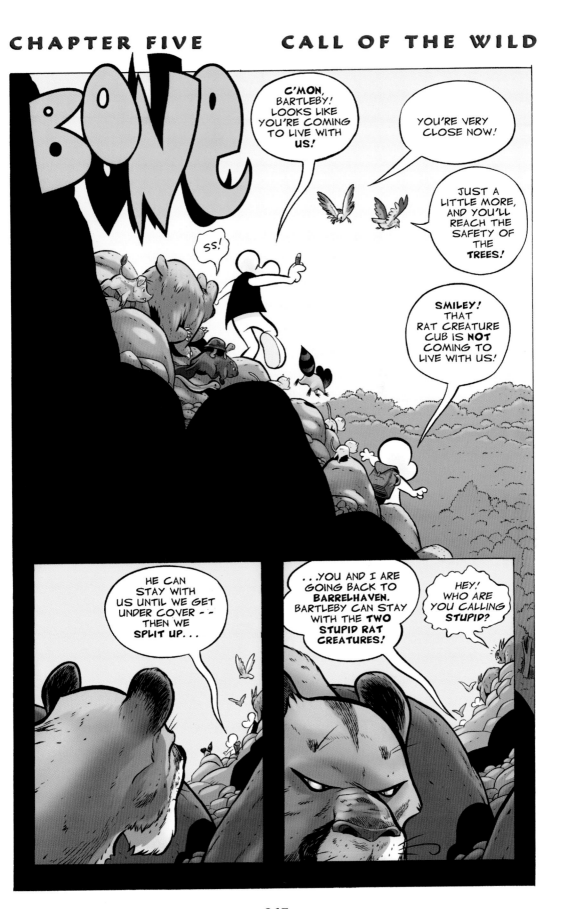

BUT, FONE BONE, THESE TWO CLOWNS CAN'T TAKE CARE OF A LITTLE **CUB!** THEY CAN'T EVEN TAKE CARE OF **THEMSELVES!**

BARTLEBY **CAN'T** LIVE IN THE VALLEY, SMILEY! HE WON'T BE **SAFE!**

SAY! SPEAKING OF THE VALLEY-- LOOK OUT THERE!

WHAT?

THAT COLUMN OF SMOKE WE SAW IS **GONE!** DO YOU THINK TH' FOREST FIRE IS OUT?

I GUESS SO. BUT I'M NOT SO SURE IT **WAS** A FOREST FIRE . . .

WHAT ELSE COULD IT HAVE BEEN?

I DON'T KNOW FOR SURE, BUT ALL OF **ROCK JAW'S** TALK ABOUT **WAR** IS MAKING ME KIND OF **NERVOUS!**

ROCK JAW! THAT OL' **BLOWHARD!** HE WAS SO FULL OF HIMSELF...

...BUT WE SHOWED THAT GIANT KITTY CAT, **DIDN'T** WE, KIDS?

YEAH! **HA!** HA!

I BET HE'S **STILL** AT THE TOP OF THE CLIFF GUARDIN' THE ENTRANCE TO THAT **CAVE!**

HEE! HEE! OL' ROCK JAW DOESN'T KNOW ABOUT OUR **SECRET TUNNEL** DOWN THROUGH THE OLD **TEMPLE!**

LET'S NOT CONGRATULATE OURSELVES JUST YET.

BESIDES, SMILEY, I'M **MUCH** MORE WORRIED ABOUT WHAT MAY HAVE HAPPENED IN THE **VALLEY** WHILE WE WERE AWAY.

OKAY, OKAY. **STILL,** I'D LIKE TO SEE THAT OL' RASCAL'S **FACE** WHEN HE REALIZES WE GAVE HIM TH' **SLIP!**

MR. BONE, IF YOU'RE WORRIED THAT SOMETHING MAY HAVE **HAPPENED** WHILE WE WERE GONE, WHY DON'T YOU ASK THE TWO **RATS** WE HAVE WITH US?

GOOD IDEA.

HEY, **YOU TWO!** WHAT DO YOU KNOW ABOUT THOSE COLUMNS OF **SMOKE** WE SAW DOWN IN THE VALLEY?

WE KNOW **NOTHING!** WE ARE ONLY LOWLY FOOT SOLDIERS ON **BORDER PATROL!**

BORDER PATROL?! THE FIRST TIME I **MET** YOU WAS ON THE OTHER SIDE OF THE VALLEY! YOU WERE DEEP IN **DRAGON TERRITORY!**

YES, YESSS, WE WERE BREAKING THE **TREATY** -- BUT **KINGDOK** COMMANDED US TO **DO IT!**

KINGDOK'S ADVISOR, **THE HOODED ONE,** TOLD HIM THAT A NEW **LEADER** WAS ENTERING THE VALLEY -- A LEADER WHO BORE A **STAR** ON HIS CHEST!

KINGDOK SENT US ACROSS THE VALLEY TO THE **DRAGON'S STAIR** TO **CAPTURE** THIS UPSTART THREAT!

THAT'S RIDICULOUS! OUR COUSIN **PHONEY BONE** IS NO LEADER! I CAN'T IMAGINE WHAT GAVE YOU GUYS THE IDEA HE WAS A **THREAT!**

ARE YOU SURE KINGDOK DIDN'T HAVE **OTHER** REASONS FOR SENDING YOU ACROSS THE VALLEY AND VIOLATING THE **TREATY?**

KINGDOK HATES THE FLAT-LANDERS, IT'S **TRUE,** BUT THE TIME WAS NOT SO LONG AGO THAT HE WAS CONTENT TO ABIDE BY THE TREATY AND LEAVE THE VALLEY DWELLERS ALONE . . .

ALL THAT CHANGED WHEN THE **HOODED ONE** ARRIVED... HE CAME TO US FROM THE VALLEY... ONE OF THE WANDERING HOLY MEN KNOWN AS **STICK-EATERS**...

...AND WITH HIM CAME THE LOCUSTS AND THE **DREAMS!**

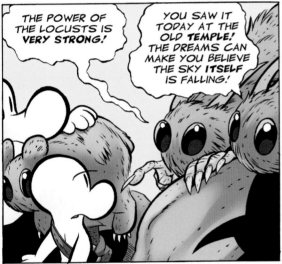

THE POWER OF THE LOCUSTS IS **VERY STRONG!**

YOU SAW IT TODAY AT THE OLD **TEMPLE!** THE DREAMS CAN MAKE YOU BELIEVE THE SKY **ITSELF** IS FALLING!

WITHOUT THE HOODED ONE TO **CONTROL** THE LOCUSTS, WE MIGHT ALL BE ROLLING SENSLESSLY ON THE GROUND, **MAD AS LOONS!**

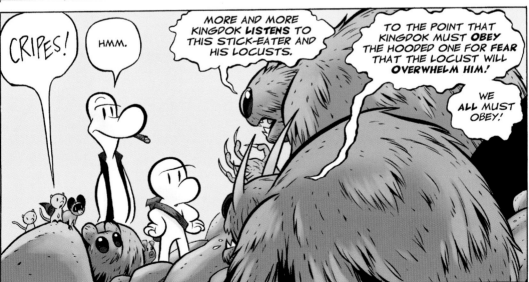

CRIPES!

HMM.

MORE AND MORE KINGDOK **LISTENS** TO THIS STICK-EATER AND HIS LOCUSTS.

TO THE POINT THAT KINGDOK MUST **OBEY** THE HOODED ONE FOR FEAR THAT THE LOCUST WILL **OVERWHELM HIM!**

WE ALL MUST OBEY!

AND **THIS** IS THE KIND OF LIFE YOU WANT TO SEND LITTLE **BARTLEBY** BACK TO? SOME KIND OF **INSECT CULT?**

BARTLEBY IS A **RAT CREATURE**, SMILEY! IF THIS IS WHAT RAT CREATURES **BELIEVE**, THEN WHO ARE WE TO JUDGE?

IT WAS NOT ALWAYS SO. IN THE OLD DAYS THE **HUM-HUM** WAS GOOD. WE WERE HAPPY.

NOW WITH THE COMING OF THE **LOCUSTS**, IT IS DIFFICULT TO TELL WHAT IS GOOD. OR WHAT IS **REAL.**

THE HOODED ONE BLAMES OUR UNHAPPINESS ON THE **VALLEY PEOPLE** AND **THE DRAGONS**, AND ON THE **TREATY** WHICH FORCES US TO LIVE IN THE MOUNTAINS.

HE SAYS WE MUST RETURN TO THE **OLD WAYS**. . . TO THE TIME BEFORE THERE **WERE** VALLEY PEOPLE . . . WHEN THERE WAS **ORDER** IN THE WORLD.

YOU DON'T HAVE TO **LISTEN** TO THE HOODED ONE.

THAT'S RIGHT, HE'S NOT EVEN **ONE** OF YOU! IF YOU ASK ME, HIS **MOTIVES** ARE PRETTY **SUSPECT!**

IF WE DO **NOT** LISTEN TO HIM . . . HOW WILL WE BE HAPPY?

ONLY WHEN YOU TRULY **UNDERSTAND** THE HOODED ONE'S MOTIVES WILL YOU LEARN THE **MEANING** OF HAPPINESS . . .

WHO. . .?

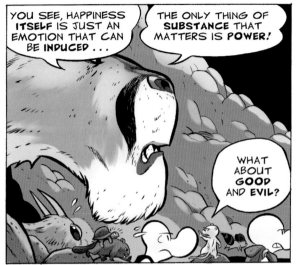

YOU SEE, HAPPINESS **ITSELF** IS JUST AN EMOTION THAT CAN BE **INDUCED** . . .

THE ONLY THING OF **SUBSTANCE** THAT MATTERS IS **POWER!**

WHAT ABOUT **GOOD** AND **EVIL?**

BAH! THERE IS NO GOOD AND EVIL. WHAT IS EVIL TO **YOU** DEPENDS ON WHAT **SIDE** YOU ARE ON. WHAT IS GOOD TO YOU IS EVIL TO THE **RAT CREATURES**, AND VICE VERSA.

THAT'S NOT **TRUE!**

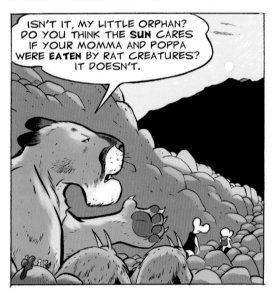

ISN'T IT, MY LITTLE ORPHAN? DO YOU THINK THE **SUN** CARES IF YOUR MOMMA AND POPPA WERE **EATEN** BY RAT CREATURES? IT DOESN'T.

THE SUN WILL **SET** TONIGHT AND **RISE AGAIN** TOMORROW WHETHER YOU AND I ARE HERE OR NOT.

ANYTHING **THESE** MISERABLE WRETCHES DO IS **UTTERLY** INSIGNIFICANT.

THERE IS NO GOOD OR EVIL. . . ONLY **NATURE.** AND IN NATURE, THE ONLY THING THAT MATTERS IS **POWER!**

CALL OF THE WILD

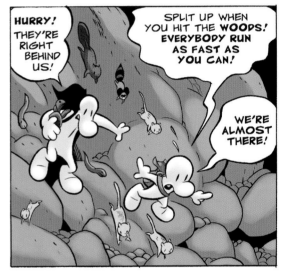

GOOD-BYE, 'POSSUMS! I'LL MISS YOU!

AREN'T YOU COMING WITH US?

NO, I LIVE IN THE MOUNTAINS. I'M STAYING HERE

THEN GOOD LUCK, RODERICK! THANKS FOR THE ADVENTURE!

YEAH, WE HAD A GREAT TIME!

HEY, YOU DORKS! YOU BETTER BREAK IT UP AN' GO HOME, OR YOU'RE GONNA BE SOMEBODY'S SUPPER!

GOODBYE FOR NOW! COME BACK TO TH' MOUNTAINS AN' VISIT ME!

WE WILL, RODERICK! GOODBYE!

GOODBYE!

GOODBYE!

THEY CAN'T JUST VANISH INTO **THIN AIR!**

YOU THINK IT WAS ANOTHER **DREAM?!**

NO - - WAIT! **THERE THEY ARE!** UP THERE!

THEY'RE **LEAVING!** AN' THEY'RE CARRYING KINGDOK AWAY!

G#ϟ!!

LOOK AT **THAT!** THERE'S TWO GUYS RUNNIN' UP BEHIND THEM!

IT'S THE **TWO STUPID RAT CREATURES!**

THOSE **BACKSTABBERS!** THEY TRIED TO HAND US OVER AT TH' LAST MOMENT!

THERE HE IS!

WHAT'S HE DOIN'?!

HE'S TRYING TO REJOIN THE GROUP, TOO!

BUT I DON'T WANT HIM TO REJOIN TH' GROUP!

IT'S WHERE HE BELONGS, SMILEY! IT'S WHAT HE WANTS TO DO!

MMMMMM.

DON'T BE SAD! IT'S WHAT WE CAME HERE TO DO! THIS IS A HAPPY ENDING!

NATURE HAS TAKEN ITS COURSE!

WILL HE BE OKAY?

YEAH. YEAH. HE'LL BE FINE.

LISTEN . . .

YOU CAN WATCH HIM FOR A WHILE IF YOU WANT, BUT NOT TOO LONG -- WE GOTTA GO, ALL RIGHT?

I GUESS.

GOOD-BYE, BARTLEBY.

I GOTTA GO NOW.

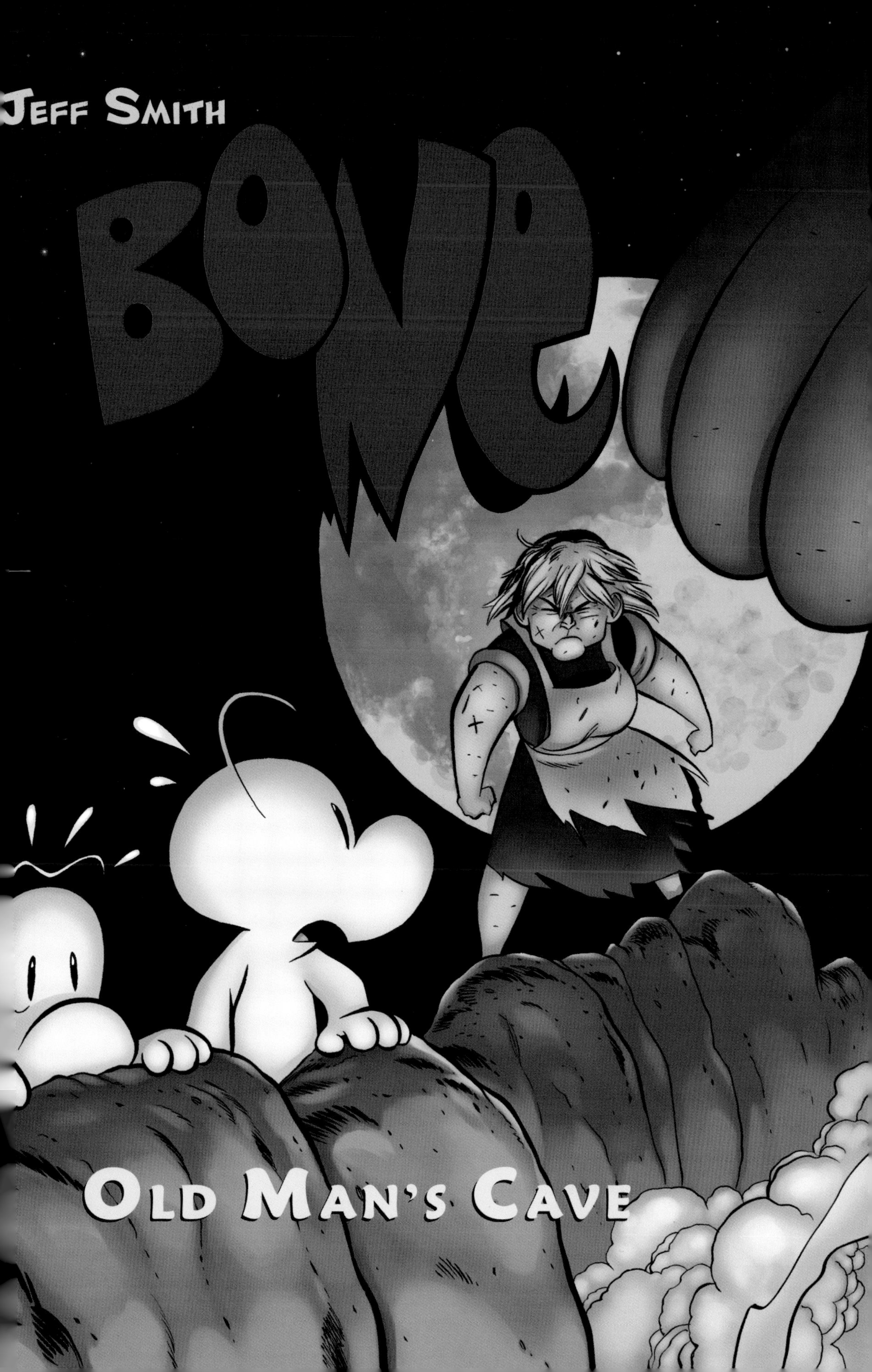
Jeff Smith
BONE
Old Man's Cave

This book is for Jim Kammerud

YEAH, I SAID **FONE BONE**, AN' THIS IS **HIM**.

oh! oh! OH, MY! YOU'RE TH' ONE THEY'RE LOOKIN' FOR!!! THE ONE WHO **KILLED KINGDOK**!!

KILLED KINGDOK? WHAT'RE YOU TALKING ABOUT? I DIDN'T KILL ANYBODY.

STAY AWAY FROM ME! YOU GUYS ARE **TROUBLE!**

BUT **WAIT!** I DIDN'T KILL KINGDOK, I **SWEAR** -- HOW COULD I? HE'S **GIGANTIC!**

BESIDES, THE LAST TIME WE SAW **THAT** DUDE, HE WAS **ALIVE!**

THAT'S NOT WHAT **I** HEARD.

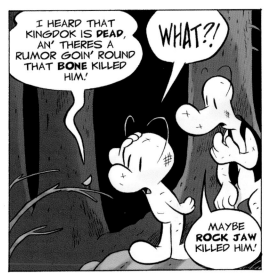

I HEARD THAT KINGDOK IS **DEAD**, AN' THERES A RUMOR GOIN' ROUND THAT **BONE** KILLED HIM!

WHAT?!

MAYBE **ROCK JAW** KILLED HIM!

YEAH! YEAH! WE SAW A GIANT MOUNTAIN LION NAMED ROQUE JA **ATTACK** KINGDOK A FEW DAYS AGO!

TORE HIM UP PRETTY GOOD, TOO. BUT HE WAS **ALIVE** AFTER THAT...

IS **THORN** OKAY? IS EVERYTHING ALL RIGHT?

FROM THE TOP OF THE MOUNTAIN WE SAW COLUMNS OF **SMOKE** COMING FROM THE FOREST...

IT'S **BAD**, BONE -- **REAL** BAD. THAT'S WHY I BEEN LOOKIN' FOR YOU...

TELL ME! IS SHE OKAY?

LAST I SAW THORN SHE WAS RESCUING THE GREAT RED DRAGON FROM PHONEY BONE'S **LYNCH MOB.**

OH NO!

I **KNEW IT!** I **KNEW IT** HAD SOMETHING TO DO WITH PHONEY! **WHAT HAPPENED?**

THORN **SAVED THE** DRAGON, BUT AT THAT VERY **SAME MOMENT,** THE RAT CREATURES **INVADED** THE VALLEY!

THAT'S TH' **SMOKE** YOU SAW! THOSE MONSTERS ARE BURNING EVERY FARM IN THEIR **PATH!**

OHMYGOSH.

LUCKILY, AIN'T NOBODY BEEN **KILT** YET, AS FAR AS I **KNOWS,** BUT LOTSA FOLKS IS **HOMELESS** AN' **SCARED!**

WAIT'LL I GET MY HANDS ON THAT **NO-GOOD, SELFISH COUSIN** OF OURS -- HIM AND THAT **STUPID STAR SHIRT** HE ALWAYS WEARS!

EVER SINCE WE **CAME** TO THIS VALLEY THE RAT CREATURES HAVE BEEN SEARCHING FOR *THE ONE WHO BEARS THE STAR* --

-- BECAUSE **THEY** THINK PHONEY'S A **THREAT** TO THEM, AN' NOW THEY'RE SEARCHING FOR **YOU** CAUSE THEY THINK YOU KILLED **KINGDOK!**

YOU KNOW WHAT THE **WORST** THING IS? BECAUSE OF **US,** THE ENEMY KNOWS **THORN** IS A MEMBER OF THE LOST ROYAL FAMILY. NOW **SHE'S** IN DANGER, TOO.

MAYBE THAT GROUNDHOG WAS RIGHT. WE **ARE** TROUBLE!

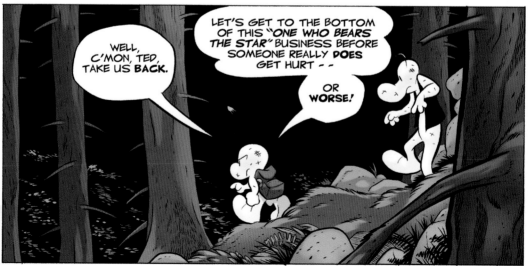

WELL, C'MON, TED, TAKE US **BACK.**

LET'S GET TO THE BOTTOM OF THIS *"ONE WHO BEARS THE STAR"* BUSINESS BEFORE SOMEONE REALLY **DOES** GET HURT --

OR **WORSE!**

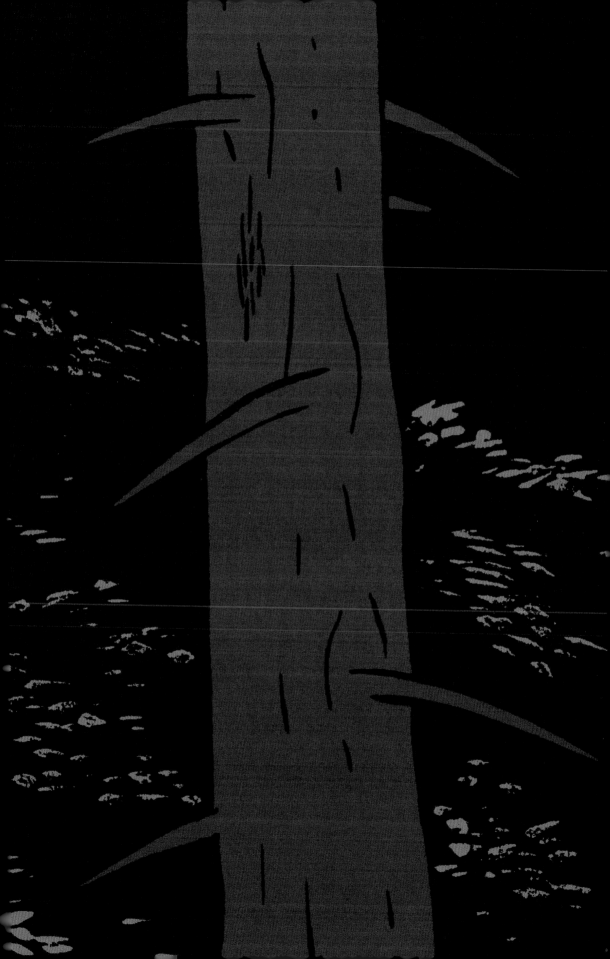

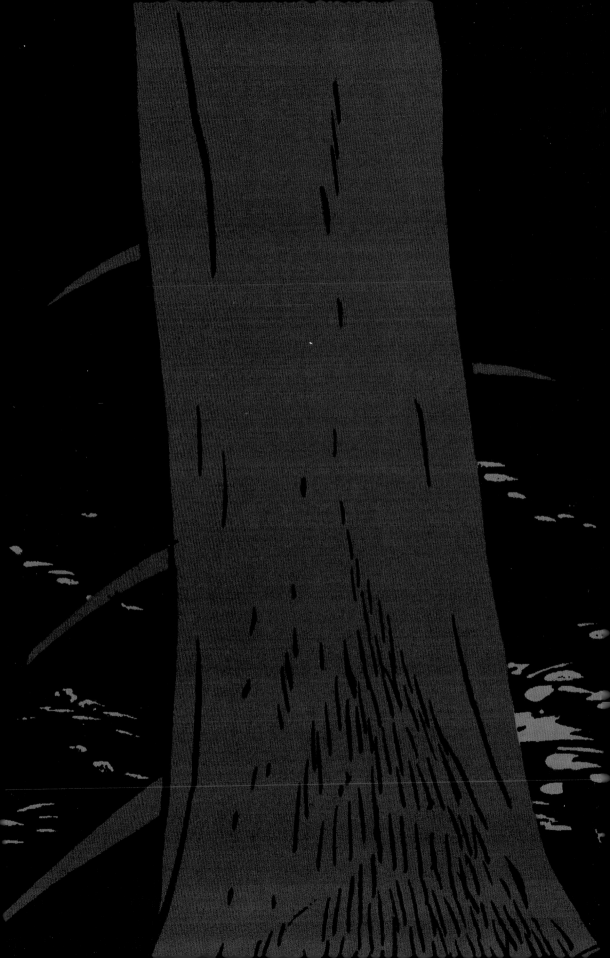

RUMORS ARE RUNNING WILD UP AND DOWN THE FRONT LINES THAT **KINGDOK IS DEAD!**

?!!

Shoss! NESSEN! NESSEN!

IK GAREN SPEK NESSEN!

WHAT ARE THEY SAYING? I DON'T UNDERSTAND.

Shh!

WELL, **I** UNDERSTOOD 'EM **PLENTY!** THEY'RE LOOKIN' FOR A **BALD CREATURE** WHO BEARS A **STAR!** SOUND LIKE ANYBODY YOU KNOW?!

WENDELL! KEEP QUIET!

I KNEW YOU WERE NO GOOD, BONE! I SHOULDA LISTENED TO **LUCIUS!** JUST WAIT'LL WE GET BACK TO TOWN, YOU RUNT, I'LL FIX YOU **GOOD!**

THEY ARE TURNING AROUND. HEADING BACK **EAST!**

WHAT TH' HECK WAS **THAT** ALL ABOUT? THEY SEEMED PRETTY **UPSET** ABOUT SOMETHING!

THEY'RE IN A STATE OF **CONFUSION**--

THERE ARE RUMORS THEIR CHIEFTAIN HAS BEEN **KILLED.**

ALL THE PATROL TEAMS ARE RETURNING TO THEIR BASE CAMPS TO FIND OUT WHAT IS GOING ON.

HOW CAN YOU TELL **THAT?** THEY WERE TALKING IN SOME KIND OF **JIBBERISH!**

THEY WERE SPEAKING **NESSEN** . . . AN ANCIENT RAT CREATURE LANGUAGE RESERVED FOR TIMES OF WAR AND MILITARY EMERGENCY.

OH, REALLY? AND WHEN DID YOU LEARN TO SPEAK AN ANCIENT RAT CREATURE **MILITARY LANGUAGE?!**

I **DIDN'T.** BUT FOR SOME REASON I UNDERSTOOD EVERY SINGLE WORD THEY SAID.

MRS. TANNER, WE HAVE SOME FOOD AND WATER FOR YOUR FAMILY AT A SMALL CAMP NOT FAR FROM HERE...

...THAT'S WHERE THE REST OF THE VILLAGERS ARE. WE'RE GOING TO SEND YOU BACK THERE UNTIL WE CAN DETERMINE THAT THE TOWN IS SAFE.

WHY IS THIS **HAPPENING**, THORN? WHY ARE THE HAIRY MEN **DOING** THIS?

WE'RE TRYING TO FIND OUT.

I THINK WE KNOW **ENOUGH!** LET'S STRING THE LITTLE RUNT UP **RIGHT NOW!**

NO. WE'RE GOING TO THE **TOWN.** IT'S A CLOUDLESS NIGHT, SO WE'LL KEEP TO THE RAVINES. SAM CAN TAKE THE TANNERS BACK TO OUR CAMP. JON, WENDELL AND EUCLID, YOU KNOW THE ROUTINE. **LET'S GO.**

I **SWEAR** I DON'T KNOW WHAT THE RAT CREATURES WANT, THORN! THIS IS ALL SOME KINDA CRAZY **MIX-UP!**

THEY'RE NOT JUST AFTER **ME,** THEY'RE AFTER SOME **PRINCESS!** I'M **INNOCENT,** THORN! YA GOTTA BELIEVE ME!

I **DO** BELIEVE YOU. THAT'S THE **ONLY** REASON I HAVEN'T LET WENDELL AND EUCLID STRING YOU UP.

YOU-- YOU **MEAN** IT? YOU BELIEVE ME?

YES, I DO. WOULD YOU BELIEVE **ME** IF I SAID THE PRINCESS WAS INNOCENT, TOO?

NOW LET'S GO SEE WHAT'S LEFT OF OUR TOWN.

STOP ACTING LIKE AN **ANIMAL.** HASN'T THERE BEEN ENOUGH VIOLENCE? NOW PUT PHONEY BONE **DOWN.**

NO!! HE SWINDLED US AND **DESTROYED** OUR TOWN!

HE DIDN'T ATTACK THE VILLAGE! THE **RAT CREATURES** DID!

HE TRICKED US INTO CHASIN' AFTER **DRAGONS!** WE WERE AWAY FROM OUR **HOMES** WHEN WE SHOULDA BEEN **HERE** DEFENDING THE **VILLAGE!**

NOBODY **FORCED** YOU TO FOLLOW HIM! YOU WERE A **MOB** LOOKING FOR SCAPEGOATS!

BUT IF WE HAD BEEN **HERE,** THEN LUCIUS MIGHT STILL BE **ALIVE!**

WE DON'T KNOW WHAT HAPPENED TO LUCIUS. . . BUT WHATEVER IT WAS, IF YOU **HAD** BEEN HERE, YOU WOULD HAVE **SHARED** HIS FATE!

AND SO WOULD ALL THE OTHER VILLAGERS WHO WERE **WITH** YOU HUNTING DRAGONS! THIS BONE PROBABLY SAVED **HALF THE VILLAGE** BY TAKING YOU UP INTO THE MOUNTAINS!

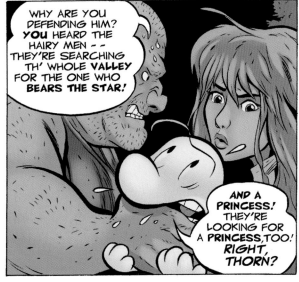

WHY ARE YOU DEFENDING HIM? **YOU** HEARD THE HAIRY MEN -- THEY'RE SEARCHING TH' WHOLE **VALLEY** FOR THE ONE WHO **BEARS THE STAR!**

AND A **PRINCESS!** THEY'RE LOOKING FOR A **PRINCESS, TOO!** RIGHT, THORN?

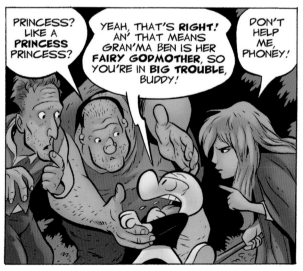

A **PRINCESS**? **HOW**? FROM **WHERE**?! THE ROYAL FAMILY WAS KILLED IN THE BIG **WAR**!

THERE HASN'T BEEN A KINGDOM FOR ALMOST **FIFTEEN YEARS**!

YES, I KNOW THAT. **EVERYBODY** KNOWS THAT -- EXCEPT, APPARENTLY, FOR THE **RAT CREATURES** AND MY **GRAN'MA BEN**. THEY DEFINITELY THINK I'M A PRINCESS.

BUT THAT DOESN'T MEAN I **AM** A PRINCESS NECESSARILY--

SHE DOES KINDA **LOOK** LIKE A PRINCESS.

YES, BUT WHAT DOES THAT MAKE OL' **ROSE BEN**? THE LOST QUEEN OF THE **VALLEY**? OL' GRAN'MA BEN RACES **COWS**, REMEMBER. . .

LOOK, I DON'T KNOW IF IT'S TRUE. . . BUT I **AM** SURE WE SHOULDN'T BE DISCUSSING IT **HERE**!

THAT MEANS **YOU** CAN JUST KEEP YOUR **TRAP SHUT** -- UNDERSTAND?

YEAH, YEAH. WE ALL GOT OUR LITTLE **DELUSIONS OF GRANDEUR**. I COULD TELL YOU WANTED TO GET IT OFF YOUR CHEST.

LISTEN UP. THIS WAR CLUB BELONGS TO MY FRIEND **FONE BONE**. I FOUND IT HERE IN THE WRECKAGE OF THE BARN, AND THERE'S A GOOD CHANCE HE AND SOME OTHERS **ESCAPED**. . .

"I HAVE GONE HOME TO GRAN'MA'S FARM."

I WROTE THIS THE NIGHT I LEFT THE COMPOUND SO FONE BONE WOULD KNOW WHERE I WENT...

Dear Fone Bone, I have gone home to Gran'ma's farm. Please don't worry -- Just need to sort things out. If you leave the valley before we see other... bye.

LUCIUS MUST'VE **FOUND** THE NOTE.

AND HE PUT IT IN THE TREE FOR **YOU** TO FIND, JON.

WHY?

SNIFF.

WAIT! I KNOW!

BECAUSE **HE** WENT TO GRAN'MA BEN'S FARM TO LOOK FOR **THORN!**

BLOODY STARS!!

IF HE'S **RIGHT**, THEN LUCIUS MIGHT STILL BE **ALIVE!**

YEAH! MAYBE **ALL** OUR NEIGHBORS ARE STILL ALIVE!

FIRST THING IN THE MORNING, WE HEAD NORTH TO GRAN'MA BEN'S PLACE.

RIGHT!

YOU GO.

I HAVE TO LOOK FOR FONE BONE. WILL YOU BE COMING WITH ME, PHONCIBLE?

WHO **ME?** YOU MEAN OUT **THERE?!**

GULP. EEH. YEAH... I'LL GO...

WELL, AT LEAST YOU'RE NOT A **COWARD!**

OR ARE YOU **MORE** AFRAID TO BE LEFT WITH **THEM?**

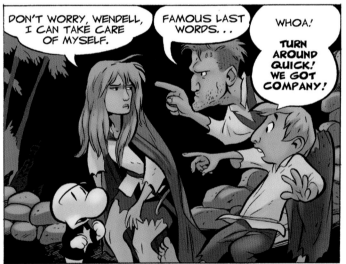

STICK-EATERS!

UM . . .
I THINK THIS MIGHT BE
FOR ME.

HELLO?

CAN I
HELP YOU?

WE BRING A
MESSAGE
TO YOU
FROM YOUR
GRANDMOTHER.

SHE IS
WAITING FOR
YOU AT OLD
MAN'S CAVE.

SHE BIDS
YOU TO
JOIN HER
IMMEDIATELY.

OLD MAN'S CAVE...

HOW DO I KNOW I CAN TRUST YOU?

BEFORE I CAN GO TO OLD MAN'S CAVE, I MUST FIND MY FRIEND **FONE BONE**.

YOUR GRANDMOTHER BIDS YOU TO JOIN HER **IMMEDIATELY**.

HELP ME FIND MY FRIEND **FIRST**.

YOU **HAVE** TO HELP ME, DON'T YOU? IT IS YOUR **DUTY**.

WE ARE BUT GUIDES.

YOU ALONE MAY WALK YOUR PATH.

THEN GUIDE ME. SHOULD I SEARCH FOR MY **FRIEND**? OR SHOULD I GO TO **OLD MAN'S CAVE**?

YOUR FRIEND WAS LAST SEEN **FAR AWAY** IN THE EASTERN MOUNTAINS. HE IS RUMORED TO HAVE BEEN INVOLVED IN THE DEATH OF THE MIGHTY **KINGDOK**, AND MANY ARMIES ARE NOW **SEARCHING** FOR HIM. . .

oh, my!

BUT REMEMBER. . . YOU HAVE A **GREATER** DUTY TO YOUR PEOPLE.

CHOOSE, YOUNG ONE. TIME IS SHORT.

WHAT DO I **DO**?

I HAVE NO IDEA.

FONE BONE WOULD KNOW.

YOUR **MAJESTY**, OLD MAN'S CAVE IS ON THE WAY TO YOUR GRANDMOTHER'S **FARM**! WE SHOULD GO THERE! PERHAPS LUCIUS AND THE OTHERS ARE ALREADY THERE **WAITING** FOR US!

I DON'T KNOW. IT'S SO HARD TO THINK. I'LL DECIDE IN THE MORNING.

YOU HEARD THE **PRINCESS**! WE'RE STOPPING FOR THE NIGHT! **JON**, YOU HAVE THE FIRST WATCH!

YES, SIR!

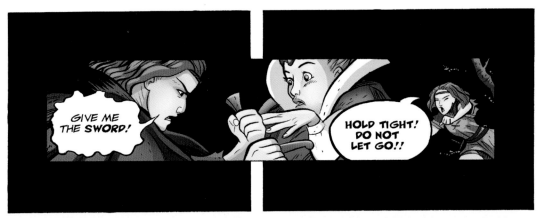

THORN COULD'VE FOUND HER WAY THROUGH THIS RAIN. **SHE COULD FIND HER WAY IN TH' DARKEST NIGHT** LIKE SHE WAS FOLLOWING A MAP.

YES, SHE COULD. IT'S **UNCANNY.**

hmmf.

SHE FOLLOWS THE **DRAGONS IN THE EARTH.** JUST LIKE TH' DRAGON TOLD HER.

YEAH, WELL, SHE'S FOLLOWIN' DRAGONS **SOMEWHERE ELSE! FORGET HER!** WE GOT PROBLEMS OF OUR OWN--

HEY!

THAT'S IT-- I'VE **HAD IT!**

SPLOSH!

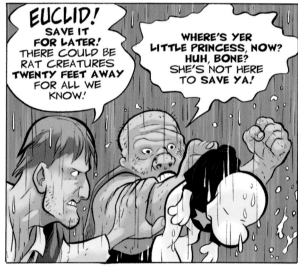

EUCLID! SAVE IT FOR LATER! THERE COULD BE RAT CREATURES **TWENTY FEET AWAY** FOR ALL WE KNOW!

WHERE'S YER **LITTLE PRINCESS, NOW? HUH, BONE?** SHE'S NOT HERE TO SAVE YA!

PUT HIM **DOWN,** EUCLID!

STAY BACK! I'VE **HAD** IT WITH THIS **TROUBLEMAKER!** **THIS IS ALL HIS FAULT!**

ALL RIGHT, THAT'S ENOUGH. I DON'T KNOW WHERE THORN **IS,** BUT UNTIL SHE GETS BACK, **I'M ENFORCING HER ORDERS!**

YOU'RE A **FOOL,** WENDELL! SHE RAN OUT ON US LAST NIGHT! WHAT DO YOU **CARE** WHAT SHE WANTS?!

I CARE BECAUSE SHE'S A **HARVESTAR!**

THE HARVESTARS WERE WIPED OUT **FIFTEEN YEARS** AGO WHEN ATHEIA WAS **SACKED!** THERE'S NOBODY **ALIVE** WITH THAT NAME!

THERE'VE BEEN RUMORS FOR **YEARS** THAT THE LITTLE GIRL SURVIVED THE **MASSACRE--**

YEAH, **I** KNOW, AN' OL' GRAN'MA BEN IS TH' **LOST QUEEN OF TH' VALLEY!**

HALT!

WHO'S THERE?

THERE'S A WAR ON, GENTLEMEN. **CONTROL** YOURSELVES . . .

. . . OR I'LL PICK YOU **BOTH** UP, AN' KNOCK SOME **SENSE** INTO YOU.

GRAN'MA BEN -- !

WHERE'S MY GRANDDAUGHTER? WHERE'S **THORN?**

SHE WAS WITH US LAST NIGHT, BUT WE GOT UP THIS MORNING, AND SHE WAS **GONE.**

I'LL FIND HER.

LUCIUS! YOU'RE **ALIVE!**

COME WITH ME. WE'RE NEAR THE CAVE NOW, AND YOU CAN DRY OFF - -

TH - THAT'S AMAZING.

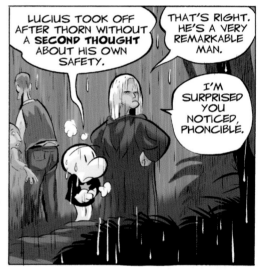

LUCIUS TOOK OFF AFTER THORN WITHOUT A **SECOND THOUGHT** ABOUT HIS OWN SAFETY.

THAT'S RIGHT. HE'S A VERY REMARKABLE MAN.

I'M SURPRISED YOU NOTICED, PHONCIBLE.

COME. IT'S NOT SAFE OUT HERE, YOU'LL CATCH YOUR **DEATH.**

I'M F-FREEZING, FONE BONE... CAN'T WE STOP FOR A **MINUTE**?

WE GOTTA KEEP **MOVIN'**, SMILEY.

TRY TO KEEP YOUR MIND ON OTHER THINGS!

BUT I'M GETTIN' SO SLEEPY...

PINCH YOURSELF --

WE HAVE TO GET BACK! I'M WORRIED THAT SOMETHING **BAD** HAS HAPPENED!

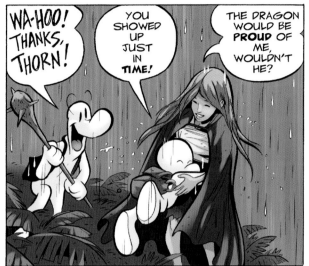

WA-HOO! THANKS, THORN!

YOU SHOWED UP JUST IN **TIME!**

THE DRAGON WOULD BE **PROUD** OF ME, WOULDN'T HE?

I'LL SAY! THAT RESCUE WAS AS **LAST MINUTE** AS ANY THE **DRAGON** EVER MADE -- ANY DAY!

HA HA!

GOSH, IT'S GOOD TO SEE YOU AGAIN.

YOU TOO. AND I'M PROBABLY GOING TO GET IN **BIG TROUBLE** FOR COMING.

HIYA, **THORNY!** IT'S **ME**, TED TH' **BUG!** WHY'S YOU GONNA GET IN **TROUBLE** FOR?

GRAN'MA BEN WANTED ME TO MEET HER AT **OLD MAN'S CAVE.** SHE'S LOOKING FOR ME.

SPEAKING OF WHICH, WE BETTER GET MOVING.

WE'RE KINDA **LOST.** EVEN TED CAN'T TELL WHICH WAY IS WHICH IN THIS **RAIN!**

YEAH, THORNY. WHICH WAY IS OL' MAN'S CAVE FROM HERE?

WELL, LET'S SEE. . .

THAT WAY. OLD MAN'S CAVE IS DIRECTLY THAT WAY.

WOW! WE WERE HEADING IN TH' WRONG DIRECTION!

GREAT! LET'S GET GOIN'! GRAN'MA'S AWAITIN' ON US!

HEY, THORN! YOU'RE GOING THE WRONG WAY! YOU JUST SAID OLD MAN'S CAVE IS **THIS** WAY!

WE'RE NOT GOING TO OLD MAN'S CAVE. THERE'S NOBODY THERE WE CAN **TRUST**.

NOW, C'MON. WE NEED TO FIND SHELTER.

I **MUST** HAVE A PARTNER TO TIP THE BALANCE . . .

TWO TOGETHER ARE NECESSARY TO PERFORM THE RITUAL . . . YOU KNOW THIS . . .

USE THE GIRL.

IF YOU TRULY WISHED TO FREE US . . .

YOU WOULD HAVE BROUGHT THE PRINCESS BEFORE US . . .

MANY ATTEMPTS HAVE BEEN MADE TO REACH THE **VENI-YAN-CARI** . . . BUT SHE HAS AWAKENED AND REPELS OUR CALLS . . .

ALSO . . .

THERE ARE **OTHER** WAYS TO SHIFT THE - -

SILENCE!

ENOUGH ABOUT THIS STAR BEARER!

MASTER . . .
PLEASE DO NOT BE ANGRY . . .
OUR PLAN IS **WORKING!**

OUR MILITARY OBJECTIVE . . . TO
CAUSE WIDESPREAD FEAR AND
PANIC HAS BEEN ACCOMPLISHED . . .
WE HAVE SWEPT ACROSS THE VALLEY
AND BACK . . . DESTROYING EVERY
FARM IN OUR PATH . . .

THE FLAT-LANDERS ARE
BECOMING DISCONNECTED . . .
THE STAR BEARER HAS **HELPED**
BY SOWING SEEDS OF DISTRUST
AGAINST THE DRAGONS!

REACH OUT!
DO YOU NOT **FEEL** IT?
THE BALANCE IS **SHIFTING!**
SOON YOU WILL BE **FREE** . . .

YES . . . IT IS
TRUE . . .
WE ARE COMING
CLOSER TO THE
SURFACE . . .

THEN HEAR ME, O LORD . . .
THE PRINCESS SURELY HAS THE
POWER TO **FREE** YOU . . .
BUT SHE ALSO HAS THE
STRENGTH TO **DESTROY YOU** --

. . . PERHAPS
YOU ARE
JEALOUS OF THE
PRINCESS AND THAT
IS WHY YOU
PREFER THE STAR
BEARER . . .

MASTER . . . I AM BUT
YOUR HUMBLE SERVANT . . .
I MERELY PROPOSE THAT THE
VENI-YAN-CARI IS MORE
POWERFUL AND POSES
A GREATER **RISK**
SHOULD IT BECOME
NECESSARY TO PERFORM
A **SACRIFICE** . . .

AND SHE
WOULD
TAKE YOUR
PLACE AS OUR
EYES AND
HANDS . . .

PLEASE . . . MY LORD,
IF YOU COULD SEE THE **OMEN** . . .
YOU WOULD KNOW THAT THE
ONE WHO BEARS THE STAR
IS A VENI-YAN-CARI . . .
THE TWO OF US **WILL** BE
ABLE TO SHIFT THE DREAMING
. . . AND WITH LESS
RISK TO YOURSELF.

YES . . .
YOU ARE RIGHT . . .

YES . . .

FOR NOW
AT LEAST . . .
YOU ARE OUR
EYES . . .

WOULD YOU GUYS MIND KEEPIN' IT **DOWN** IN HERE?

OOPS! SORRY, TED.

AIN'T IT HARD ENOUGH I'M **PATROLLIN'** THE AREA TRYIN' TO KEEP YOU GUYS **UN-SEEN**, YOU GOTTA GO ALL WHOOPIN' IT UP SO I GOTTA KEEP YA **UN-HEARD TOO**?!

OKAY, OKAY. WE'LL KEEP IT DOWN. WE PROMISE.

JUST A FEW MORE DAYS, TED, UNTIL WE FINISH OUR PLAN.

PLAN? THE ONLY THING I SEE YOU PLANNIN' IS A RAID ON TH' SURROUNDIN' **CHERRY TREES!**

THESE WARM SUMMER DAYS AIN'T GONNA LAST FOREVER, THORN. YOU DON'T **HURRY UP**, WE GONNA BE HIDIN' FROM THE RAT CREATURES IN A **SNOWBANK!**

WE'RE NOT **HIDING**. OUR PLAN IS TO **ATTACK** THE HOODED ONE.

ATTACK HIM, HUH? JES' TH' **FOUR** OF US? WE GONNA WALK RIGHT INTO TH' RAT CREATURES' CAMP AN' JES' **POP** TH' HOODED ONE ON TH' **CHOPS**?

NO, TED, OF COURSE NOT. YOU KNOW BETTER THAN THAT.

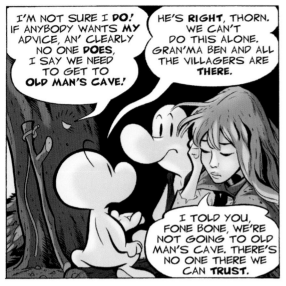

I'M NOT SURE I **DO**! IF ANYBODY WANTS **MY** ADVICE, AN' CLEARLY NO ONE **DOES**, I SAY WE NEED TO GET TO **OLD MAN'S CAVE!**

HE'S **RIGHT**, THORN. WE CAN'T DO THIS ALONE. GRAN'MA BEN AND ALL THE VILLAGERS ARE **THERE**.

I TOLD YOU, FONE BONE, WE'RE NOT GOING TO OLD MAN'S CAVE. THERE'S NO ONE THERE WE CAN **TRUST**.

YOU CAN TRUST **GRAN'MA BEN!**

I SAID NO. NOW, PLEASE GO BACK ON PATROL, AND MAKE SURE THAT ANYONE WHO COMES THIS WAY- - ANY BIRD, ANY ANIMAL, OR ANY INSECT- - **ANYONE** - - IS TURNED AWAY WITHOUT SEEING US.

ALL RIGHT, I'M **GOIN'**. BUT WHEN THIS IS ALL OVER, GRAN'MA BEN GONNA SQUISH ME LIKE A **BUG** FOR DISOBEYIN' HER.

ARE YOU **SURE** ABOUT GRAN'MA BEN? 'CAUSE TO TELL TH' **TRUTH**, I KINDA **MISS** HER.

EXCUSE ME. . . I'M GOING TO FIX SOME SUPPER. WOULD YOU MIND HANDING ME SOME OF THAT FUEL, SMILEY?

YEAH, OKAY. . . IT'S JUST THAT MAYBE I DON'T UNDERSTAND TH' **PLAN**.

COULD YOU MAKE A LITTLE PILE WITH THOSE DROPPINGS?

DROPPINGS? EEYUU!

DRIED ANIMAL DROPPINGS. MAKES A SMOKELESS FIRE.

WE CAN WORK ON OUR PLAN WHILE WE EAT.

THORN, WE DON'T **HAVE** A PLAN.

YEAH, HOW ARE WE GONNA **GET** THE HOODED ONE? WE DON'T KNOW NOTHIN' **ABOUT** HIM EXCEPT THAT HE APPEARS IN YOUR **DREAMS.**

WE KNOW HE HAS AN **ARMY** THAT'S OUT HUNTING FOR YOU AND OUR COUSIN PHONEY BONE.

YEAH, THORN, WHO **IS** THIS GUY, ANYWAY?

I DON'T KNOW. THERE'S A PROTECTIVE SPELL AROUND THE HOODED ONE SIMILAR TO THE ONE TED AND I PUT AROUND THE FOUR OF **US.**

. . . BUT I DO KNOW **SOME** THINGS.

I KNOW THE HOODED ONE DRAWS HIS POWER FROM A DREAM BEING CALLED THE **LORD OF THE LOCUSTS.**

THESE POWERS LET THE HOODED ONE TRAVEL IN - -AND IN SOME CASES EVEN **PERVERT** - - OTHER PEOPLE'S DREAMS.

THE MORE FEAR HE CAUSES, THE MORE POWERFUL HE BECOMES!

SO WHY'S HE WANT YOU AN' PHONEY?

I **BELIEVE** HE WANTS US BOTH FOR THE SAME PURPOSE... TO SPEED THE RELEASE OF HIS **MASTER**, THE LORD OF THE LOCUSTS, WHO IS TRAPPED IN **STONE**.

THE HOODED ONE THINKS YOUR COUSIN AND I HAVE THE POWER TO HELP FREE HIM.

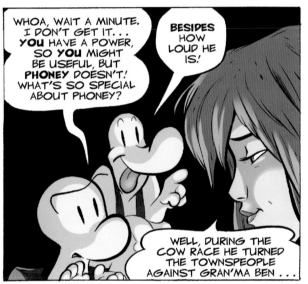

WHOA, WAIT A MINUTE. I DON'T GET IT... **YOU** HAVE A POWER, SO **YOU** MIGHT BE USEFUL, BUT **PHONEY** DOESN'T! WHAT'S SO SPECIAL ABOUT PHONEY?

BESIDES HOW LOUD HE IS!

WELL, DURING THE COW RACE HE TURNED THE TOWNSPEOPLE AGAINST GRAN'MA BEN...

THEN HE RILED UP FEAR AND ANGER AT THE **DRAGONS** FOR HIS DRAGONSLAYER SCAM!

THAT'S **EXACTLY** THE KIND OF THING THAT FEEDS THE HOODED ONE'S POWERS.

WE KNOW HE CAUSES TROUBLE, BUT --

BOY, DO WE KNOW!

WE GOT RUN OUTTA **BONEVILLE** BECAUSE PHONEY RAN FOR MAYOR...

HEE HEE! ~SNORT!~ HE CHASED ALL TH' HIGH SOCIETY **MUCKETY-MUCKS** INTO THE **RIVER** WITH A GIANT CAMPAIGN BALLOON OF HIMSELF!

IT'S NOT **FUNNY**!

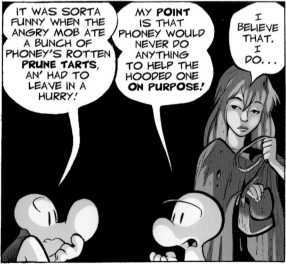

IT WAS SORTA FUNNY WHEN THE ANGRY MOB ATE A BUNCH OF PHONEY'S ROTTEN **PRUNE TARTS**, AN' HAD TO LEAVE IN A HURRY!

MY **POINT** IS THAT PHONEY WOULD NEVER DO ANYTHING TO HELP THE HOODED ONE **ON PURPOSE**!

I BELIEVE THAT. I DO...

BUT WE'RE WALKING INTO A NIGHTMARE AND WE NEED TO BE CAREFUL.

THAT'S WHY THE RAT CREATURES ARE ATTACKING THE VALLEY. EVERY FAMILY THAT IS **TERRORIZED** BRINGS HIM ONE STEP CLOSER TO THE POWER HE NEEDS TO RELEASE HIS **MASTER.**

WHY WOULD **ANYBODY** WANT TO RELEASE THE LORD OF THE LOCUSTS?

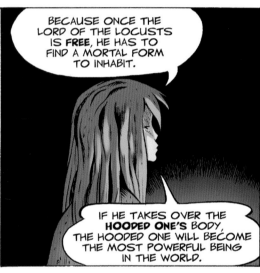

BECAUSE ONCE THE LORD OF THE LOCUSTS IS **FREE**, HE HAS TO FIND A MORTAL FORM TO INHABIT.

IF HE TAKES OVER THE **HOODED ONE'S** BODY, THE HOODED ONE WILL BECOME THE MOST POWERFUL BEING IN THE WORLD.

. . . LORD OF A NIGHTMARE EARTH.

!

THAT'S IT, THORN. PACK YOUR STUFF. WE'RE GOING TO OLD MAN'S CAVE **RIGHT NOW!** THIS IS **CRAZY,** SITTING OUT HERE!

I DON'T TRUST GRAN'MA BEN.

WHY DON'T YOU TRUST HER?! JEEZ, THORN! YOU'RE **FREAKING ME OUT!**

YOU REMEMBER THE STORY GRAN'MA TOLD US ABOUT THE NIGHT MY PARENTS WERE KILLED?

OF COURSE I DO! YOU AND YOUR PARENTS WERE ATTACKED BY **RAT CREATURES**. THE NURSEMAID BETRAYED YOU TO **KINGDOK**.

YES. WE WERE BETRAYED.

I KNOW MANY OF MY CHILDHOOD MEMORIES WERE HIDDEN FROM ME BY GRAN'MA BEN AND THE DRAGONS, BUT A LOT HAVE **RETURNED**. . .

AND THERE IS ONE THING I'M **SURE** OF- -

WE HAD NO NURSEMAID.

SKRIT!

WHO IS THERE?

COME, COME. IT IS NO USE HIDING. I KNOW YOU ARE THERE.

WHO DARES TO TRESPASS ON **ROQUE JA'S** MOUNTAIN?

... HAIL, MASTER OF THE EASTERN BORDER ...

WELL! ISN'T THIS A SURPRISE! THE HOODED ONE HIMSELF.

WHAT PURPOSE BRINGS THE MIGHTY LEADER OF THE **RAT CREATURE TRIBES** TO VISIT MY HUMBLE DOMAIN?

HUMILITY DOES NOT SUIT YOU, LION ...

I HAVE TRAVELED FAR TO ASK A **BOON** OF YOU ...

YOU ASK A FAVOR OF **ME?** **BAH!** YOUR JOURNEY HAS BEEN IN **VAIN**, HOLY ONE --

THE TIME FOR **ALLIANCES** IS PAST. YOUR LACKEY **KINGDOK** SHOULD HAVE DELIVERED **THAT** MESSAGE TO YOU ...

OR PERHAPS HE DIDN'T HAVE ENOUGH OF HIS **THROAT** LEFT TO SPEAK WITH!

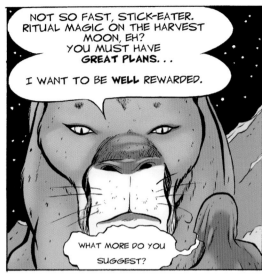

PROTECTION SPELL

JON, **PLEASE** TELL ME GRAN'MA BEN ISN'T QUEEN OF THE VALLEY! PLEASE--

oh, I'M BEGGIN' YA, MAN..

I COMMAND YOU TO TAKE A WALK WITH ME.

UM. SORRY.

SHE'S TH' QUEEN.

GAH-- MY LIFE IS GONNA SUCK, ISN'T IT?

NOW, PHONCIBLE, IT'S NOT **THAT** BAD. I'LL TELL YOU WHAT; IF YOU AGREE TO BEHAVE YOURSELF, **I** PROMISE NOT TO HAVE YOUR HEAD CUT OFF.

ho,ho! THAT'S **RICH**, I'LL SAY.

SO WHAT'S THE **DEAL** WITH ALL THESE MYSTIC WARRIORS? THIS PLACE LOOKS LIKE AN **ARMY CAMP**.

THIS PLACE IS A **SANCTUARY**. IT IS THE CENTER OF ALL THAT IS **TRANSCENDENT** IN THIS WORLD.

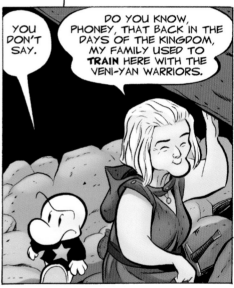

YOU DON'T SAY.

DO YOU KNOW, PHONEY, THAT BACK IN THE DAYS OF THE KINGDOM, MY FAMILY USED TO **TRAIN** HERE WITH THE VENI-YAN WARRIORS.

OH, YEAH? TRAIN FOR WHAT?

TO BE IN TWO WORLDS AT ONCE. . . TO BE **HERE**, IN OUR WORLD, AND AT THE SAME TIME IN THE **DREAMING**.

AND HOW DO YOU DO THAT?

BY CONCENTRATING ON OUR KINSHIP WITH THE REST OF CREATION.

THE DREAMING IS A GREAT RIVER THAT FLOWS AROUND US IN ALL DIRECTIONS . . .

WHEN WE **DREAM**, WE PEER THROUGH A FOGGY GLASS INTO THE RIVER AND SEE A WORLD THAT IS CONNECTED TO ALL OTHER LIVING THINGS.

THAT DREAMING WORLD EXISTS EVEN WHEN WE ARE AWAKE.

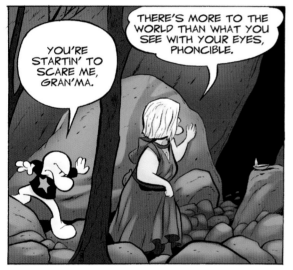

YOU'RE STARTIN' TO SCARE ME, GRAN'MA.

THERE'S MORE TO THE WORLD THAN WHAT YOU SEE WITH YOUR EYES, PHONCIBLE.

PFFF!

NOTHIN' **IMPORTANT.**

YOU ARE, WITHOUT A **DOUBT**, THE MOST MATERIALISTIC PERSON I KNOW.

COME. I WANT TO SHOW YOU SOMETHING.

A BUNCH OF **PICTURES?**

THESE PICTURES TELL A STORY. AND THIS IS THE VERY BEGINING.

BACK WHEN THE **DRAGONS** RULED THE EARTH...

WHEN THE WORLD WAS VERY, VERY NEW, THE **FIRST** DRAGON WAS A QUEEN NAMED **MIM.** MIM MAINTAINED THE DREAMING BY WATCHING ITS FLOW AND KEEPING IT **BALANCED.**

THE **DREAMING** IS A THING OF GREAT DELICACY, AND BALANCE IS MOST IMPORTANT.

MIM WATCHED THE DREAMING WITH **CARE,** AND ALL CREATURES LIVED TOGETHER IN PEACE AND HARMONY...

...UNTIL ONE DAY A SPIRIT KNOWN AS THE **LORD OF THE LOCUSTS** BECAME UNHAPPY.

THE LORD OF THE LOCUSTS WAS A NIGHTMARE BEING WITHOUT **SHAPE** OR **FORM** WHO COULD EXIST ONLY IN THE SPIRIT WORLD.

BUT HE WANTED TO MOVE IN **OUR** WORLD TOO, AND TO DO **THAT** - - TO BECOME PART OF OUR **CRUDE** REALITY - - HE WOULD HAVE TO TAKE POSSESSION OF A **MORTAL BEING'S FLESH!**

HE CHOSE **MIM, QUEEN OF THE DRAGONS,** THE MOST POWERFUL DREAMER IN THE WORLD.

DRAGONS AREN'T **IMMORTAL?**

DRAGONS LIVE FOR A VERY LONG TIME, BUT THEY ARE MORTAL. EVERYTHING IN **OUR** WORLD IS MORTAL.

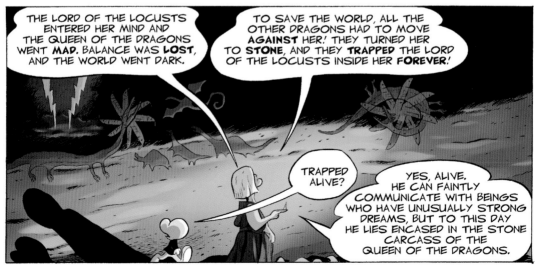

THE LORD OF THE LOCUSTS ENTERED HER MIND AND THE QUEEN OF THE DRAGONS WENT **MAD.** BALANCE WAS **LOST,** AND THE WORLD WENT DARK.

TO SAVE THE WORLD, ALL THE OTHER DRAGONS HAD TO MOVE **AGAINST** HER! THEY TURNED HER TO **STONE,** AND THEY **TRAPPED** THE LORD OF THE LOCUSTS INSIDE HER **FOREVER!**

TRAPPED ALIVE?

YES, ALIVE. HE CAN FAINTLY COMMUNICATE WITH BEINGS WHO HAVE UNUSUALLY STRONG DREAMS, BUT TO THIS DAY HE LIES ENCASED IN THE STONE CARCASS OF THE QUEEN OF THE DRAGONS.

AFTER THE FRIGHT CAUSED BY THEIR QUEEN, THE HIGH COUNCIL OF DRAGONS NO LONGER FELT THEY SHOULD BE THE SOLE GUARDIANS OF THE DREAMING...

SO THEY BEGAN TO SEARCH FOR A **HUMAN** THEY COULD TRUST, AND THEY FOUND A YOUNG GIRL NAMED **VEN**.

SHE WAS **VEN HARVESTAR**, THE FIRST QUEEN OF THE HUMANS. SHE WAS **MY** ANCESTOR, AND THORN'S ANCESTOR.

THESE COINS WERE FORGED BY THE DRAGONS AS A TOKEN OF THE COVENANT BETWEEN OUR TWO RACES TO UPHOLD AND MAINTAIN THE BALANCE OF THE **DREAMING**...

YEAH, YEAH, REAL NICE. LET'S SKIP **AHEAD** A FEW GENERATIONS. WHAT'S THIS GOT TO DO WITH **ME**?

A GREAT DEAL.

SOMEONE WANTS TO **FREE** THE LORD OF THE LOCUSTS...

WHAT?

...AND THEY NEED **YOU** TO DO IT.

ME?! WHAT FOR? I DON'T KNOW ANYTHING ABOUT **DRAGONS** OR **EVIL SPIRITS**!

THE RAT CREATURES THINK YOU DO.

IT'S A **SETUP**! I'M BEING **FRAMED**!

THE BEST INFORMATION WE HAVE IS THAT THE RAT CREATURES AND A **ROGUE** VENI-YAN WARRIOR CALLED **THE HOODED ONE** ARE SEARCHING FOR YOU IN ORDER TO FREE THE ANCIENT LORD OF THE LOCUSTS.

BUT I'M **INNOCENT!** I DON'T KNOW ANYTHING ABOUT THIS! GO GET THE **DRAGON!** YOU HAVE TO STOP THE HOODED ONE!

THE DRAGONS WON'T HELP US. THAT'S WHY I'VE GATHERED THE REMAINING **VENI-YAN** AND REOCCUPIED OLD MAN'S CAVE. IF NEED BE, WE CAN MAKE A LAST STAND HERE.

HIGHNESS--

YOUR **HIGHNESS.** LUCIUS DOWN HAS RETURNED FROM PATROL.

THANK YOU. TELL HIM WHERE TO FIND ME.

LUCIUS! GOOD OL' **LUCIUS! HE'LL** SAVE US! HE WON'T LET **ANYTHING** HAPPEN TO YOU OR THORN! HE'S **CRAZY** ABOUT YA.

YES, LUCIUS HAS ALWAYS BEEN VERY SPECIAL TO MY FAMILY.

WELL, **YOU'LL** SEE! ALL THIS **LOCUST** STUFF IS JUST A SIMPLE MISUNDERSTANDING! WE'LL GET IT ALL STRAIGHTENED OUT, THEN ME AN' MY COUSINS CAN GO **HOME,** AND YOU AN' LUCIUS CAN GET MARRIED, AND THORN CAN--

MARRIED? WHY WOULD LUCIUS AND I GET MARRIED?

BECAUSE YOU GUYS ARE OLD **SWEETHEARTS!** HE **TOLD** ME YOU TWO WERE ALMOST MARRIED ONCE.

THAT'S RIDICULOUS! LUCIUS AND I NEVER EVEN COURTED. WHY, HE WASN'T EVEN **SWEET** ON ME . . .

. . . AT LEAST NOT UNTIL IT WAS TOO LATE.

ROSE!

ANY SIGN OF MY GRANDDAUGHTER, LUCIUS? OR THE MISSING BONE BOYS?

NO, I'M SORRY.

DON'T BE. IF **ANYONE** COULD FIND THEM, IT WOULD BE YOU.

THORN IS USING ALL HER SKILLS TO THROW US OFF HER TRAIL. I'M AFRAID THE DRAGON WAS A GOOD TEACHER.

WHY WOULD THORN **WANT** TO THROW YOU OFF HER TRAIL?

I HAVEN'T EXACTLY GIVEN HER A LOT OF REASONS TO **TRUST** ME.

THERE'S MORE BAD NEWS, ROSIE. THE RAT CREATURES ARE ON THE MOVE AGAIN. THE **HOODED ONE** IS SETTING UP ENCAMPMENTS ON ALL SIDES OF US.

HOLY SMOKES!

FONE BONE'S OUT THERE!

THERE'S STILL TIME TO KEEP A PATH CLEAR TO THE SOUTH IF WE SEND A UNIT TONIGHT.

WELL, **GO! GO!** WHAT'RE YA **WAITIN'** ON, YA BIG APE?! FONE BONE AN' SMILEY ARE **OUT** THERE!

LET HIM BE, LUCIUS. HE'S JUST WORRIED ABOUT HIS COUSINS.

RRRR... IF YOU SAY SO.

YOU'RE LUCKY SOMEBODY'S LOOKIN' **OUT** FOR YOU, RUNT. OTHERWISE I'D TWIST YER SCRAWNY **NECK!**

YEAH, YEAH. I HEAR THAT A LOT LATELY.

WHO **IS** THIS HOODED ONE ANYWAY?

I WISH I KNEW.

OKAY, OKAY, JUST FOR THE SAKE OF **ARGUMENT**, SUPPOSE ALL THIS DREAM STUFF IS **REAL**...

...WHAT WOULD **ACTUALLY HAPPEN** IF THE HOODED ONE MANAGED TO SET THE **LORD OF THE LOCUSTS** FREE?

WHY, THE END OF THE WORLD, OF COURSE.

YOU ARE SO WEIRD.

CHIN UP, PHONCIBLE. WE WON'T GIVE UP THE VALLEY WITHOUT A FIGHT.

NOW IF YOU'LL EXCUSE ME, I'D BETTER GO CHECK OUR PROVISIONS.

HEY!! WATCH WHAT YOU'RE DOING! THAT'S MY **BATHWATER** YOU'RE SPILLIN'!

SINCE WHEN DO YOU LIKE TO **BATHE?** YOU'RE USUALLY LIKE A **CAT** WHEN IT COMES TO GETTING WET.

SINCE WE'VE BEEN LIVING IN THE MOUNTAINS FOR **WEEKS!** A GENTLEMAN CAN ONLY TAKE SO MUCH **CAKED-ON DIRT.**

SAY -- DO YOU HEAR THAT?

WHAT IS THAT?

SOUNDS LIKE A WOLF.

OH! BUT IT'S NOT A RAT CREATURE, THOUGH, RIGHT?

NO, IT'S JUST SOME LONELY OLD WOLF CALLING OUT INTO THE TWILIGHT.

SOUNDS KINDA SAD, DOESN'T IT?

YOU THINK HE'LL COME HERE?

THE WOLF? IF HE DOES, TED WILL TURN HIM AWAY.

C'MON, LET'S GET THIS WATER AROUND BACK.

Y'KNOW, FONE BONE, IT FEELS **GOOD** TO BE BACK AT GRAN'MA BEN'S FARMHOUSE. IT'S ALMOST LIKE BEING HOME AGAIN.

HAS THORN SAID WHAT THE **PLAN** IS? WE'RE NOT LEAVING RIGHT AWAY, ARE WE?

THAT'S THORN'S DECISION.

WELL, WHAT DOES SHE **WANT**? ARE WE GONNA STAY HERE, OR ARE WE GONNA GO TO OLD MAN'S CAVE?

I DON'T THINK SHE WANTS TO DO **EITHER**. SHE JUST WANTS TO GET SOME THINGS AND GO BACK TO THE MOUNTAINS.

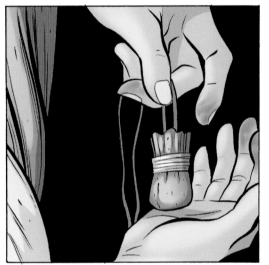

IT'S GRAN'MA BEN, ISN'T IT? THORN DOESN'T TRUST HER ANYMORE.

NOPE. SHE DOESN'T TRUST HER.

WELL, I THINK THORN'S WRONG. I THINK WE **CAN** TRUST GRAN'MA BEN, AND WE SHOULD GO MEET HER AT OLD MAN'S CAVE, LIKE TED WANTS US TO!

SO DO I . . .

...BUT UNTIL THORN CHANGES HER MIND, WE'LL JUST HAVE TO BE PATIENT.

AT LEAST UNTIL WE HEAR THIS BIG **PLAN** OF HERS.

YOU THINK SHE REALLY **HAS** A PLAN?

I SURE HOPE SO. A PLAN TO SAVE US FROM THE RAT CREATURES, **AND** TO DEAL WITH THEIR LEADER, **THE HOODED ONE.**

HMMF.

IF THORN **DID** HAVE A PLAN, WHY WOULDN'T SHE TELL IT TO US?

THE PLAN IS TO SNEAK INTO THE RAT CREATURES' ENCAMPMENT AND **ASSASSINATE** THE HOODED ONE...

THE REASON I HAVEN'T TOLD YOU ABOUT IT IS BECAUSE I'M GOING ALONE.

I'VE MADE ARRANGEMENTS WITH TED FOR THE BOTH OF YOU TO STAY HERE AT THE FARMHOUSE.

TED WILL HELP YOU FIND FOOD. YOU'LL BE SAFER HERE THAN YOU WOULD BE AT OLD MAN'S CAVE.

NOW WAIT -- WHOA, WHOA.

WHAT ARE YOU TALKING ABOUT?

YOU THINK AFTER ALL THIS, WE'RE NOT GOING TO BE PART OF THE PLAN?

ALTHOUGH I FEEL I SHOULD **STRESS** THAT IT IS A VERY **STUPID** PLAN.

THIS DOESN'T INVOLVE YOU.

IT'S **MY** PROBLEM.

DOESN'T INVOLVE ME?! THE HOODED ONE IS AFTER **MY** COUSIN PHONEY BONE! "THE ONE WHO BEARS THE STAR," **REMEMBER?**

NOT TO MENTION THAT I'VE BEEN CHASED OFF CLIFFS, PUSHED OFF WATERFALLS, **RAINED ON**, AND BEATEN UP EVERY SINGLE DAY SINCE I **GOT** TO THIS STUPID VALLEY!

WE'RE **IN**, THORN --

YOU'RE NOT MAKING THIS DECISION **WITHOUT** US!

AND BEFORE YOU SAY ANOTHER WORD -- I KNOW YOU'RE MAD AT YOUR GRANDMOTHER FOR LYING ABOUT THE DEATH OF YOUR PARENTS, BUT **MOVE ON.**

SHE THOUGHT SHE WAS PROTECTING YOU.

C'MON, THORN.

LET'S GO TO OLD MAN'S CAVE.

IT'S NOT JUST HER LIES. THERE'S MORE . . .

ALMOST EVERY NIGHT GRAN'MA BEN APPEARS TO ME IN A DREAM . . .

BUT SOMETHING IS WRONG.

SHE SEEMS SPLIT IN TWO . . .

FIRST PULLING ME IN ONE DIRECTION, THEN ANOTHER. IT'S LIKE HAVING TWO DIFFERENT GRAN'MA BENS BATTLING FOR POSSESSION OF ME.

IT'S JUST A DREAM - -

IT'S **NOT** JUST A DREAM! YOU DON'T KNOW WHAT IT'S LIKE.

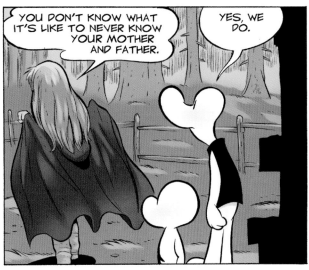

YOU DON'T KNOW WHAT IT'S LIKE TO NEVER KNOW YOUR MOTHER AND FATHER.

YES, WE DO.

WHAT DID YOU SAY?

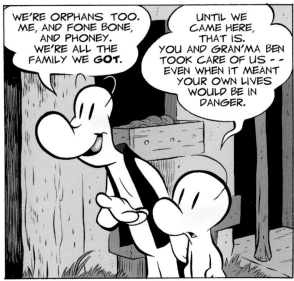

WE'RE ORPHANS TOO. ME, AND FONE BONE, AND PHONEY. WE'RE ALL THE FAMILY WE **GOT**.

UNTIL WE CAME HERE, THAT IS. YOU AND GRAN'MA BEN TOOK CARE OF US - - EVEN WHEN IT MEANT YOUR OWN LIVES WOULD BE IN DANGER.

WHEN WE WERE KIDS, PHONEY WAS THE OLDEST AND HE TOOK CARE OF US.

I ALWAYS FIGURED THAT WAS **WHY** HE GOT SO RESOURCEFUL AND STINGY.

WHEN PHONEY PULLS SOME STUPID SCAM THAT MAKES ME **CRAZY**, I KNOW DEEP DOWN HE DOESN'T MEAN TO HURT ANYONE . . .
. . . IN **HIS** MIND, HE'S STILL LOOKING OUT FOR US.

DEEP DOWN YOU KNOW IF YOU CAN TRUST SOMEONE.

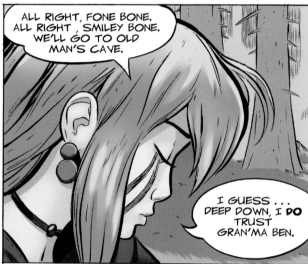

ALL RIGHT, FONE BONE. ALL RIGHT , SMILEY BONE. WE'LL GO TO OLD MAN'S CAVE.

I GUESS . . . DEEP DOWN, I **DO** TRUST GRAN'MA BEN.

GRAB YOUR STUFF, AND LET'S GO.

MAN, I HOPE YOU'RE RIGHT ABOUT THIS.'

HEY, THORN! CAN I WEAR SOME OF THAT WAR PAINT, TOO? HUH, CAN I?

HOLD UP.

THIS IS GOOD - -
WE SPLIT UP
HERE.

WENDELL, HAVE
YOUR MEN DIG IN.
REMEMBER, YOU ARE
OUR LAST LINE
OF DEFENSE - -

WE **MUST NOT**
LET THE RAT
CREATURES CROSS
THIS RIVER. IF WE DO,
OLD MAN'S CAVE
WILL BE
SURROUNDED.

CAPTAIN KNOTT, MOVE YOUR
MEN FORWARD IN A LINE
AND HOLD. WAIT FOR THE
SIGNAL.

YES,
SIR.

SCOUTS,
FOLLOW ME.

WHAT
TH - - ?

DO YOU NOT
RECOGNIZE ME?
HAS IT BEEN SO
LONG?

B - -
BRIAR?

IS IT REALLY
YOU - - ?

YES,
LUCIUS . . .
IT IS REALLY ME.
COME
CLOSER . . .

YOU CANNOT
KNOW HOW PAINFUL
IT HAS BEEN TO
BE APART FROM
YOU . . .
I HAVE
ACHED TO BE
WITH YOU . . .

TELL ME . . . HOW IS
MY BABY SISTER . . . ? HOW IS
ROSE? HAVE YOU TAKEN GOOD
CARE OF HER?

HOW SWEET IT IS TO SEE YOU . . .

HOW CAN THIS BE, BRIAR? YOU WERE **KILLED** THAT NIGHT ON THE MOUNTAIN PASS - - THE NIGHT THORN'S PARENTS WERE MURDERED. . .

ROSE SAW YOU - - YOUR BODY WAS CUT IN TWO.

IT IS TRUE . . . I DIED THAT NIGHT FIFTEEN YEARS AGO.

AND YET. . . HERE YOU ARE . . . AS BEAUTIFUL AS YOU EVER WERE IN LIFE . . .

THAT IS BECAUSE I FOUND SOMETHING **BETTER** THAN LIFE!

SNAP!

WHAT HAVE I DONE?

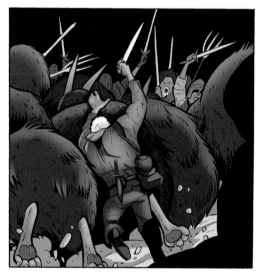

YOUR MAJESTY . . .

STILL NO WORD FROM LUCIUS DOWN.

WE'VE SENT OUT A TEAM OF WARRIORS TO RE-ESTABLISH CONTACT.

MOST OF THE VILLAGERS ARE SAFELY IN THE CAVE.

AND STILL NO SIGN OF THORN?

I THOUGHT NOT.

PLEASE KEEP THE CAMP ON ALERT, CAPTAIN.

NOW WHERE WERE WE, PHONCIBLE?

YOU WERE TALKING ABOUT MY SOUL.

AH, YES, YOUR SOUL IS THAT BIT OF THE DREAMING THAT MAKES YOU YOU.

YEAH, YEAH. EVERYTHING'S A BIG DREAM TO YOU, ISN'T IT, ROSE?

EACH OF US, IN FACT, IS A SMALL CONCENTRATED BIT OF DREAM CARRIED ALONG IN THE CURRENTS OF THE GREAT DREAMING RIVER THAT FLOWS ALL AROUND US.

WITHIN OURSELVES . . . THE DREAMING MAY FLOW IN MANY DIRECTIONS. BUT OCCASIONALLY THERE IS ONE BORN WITHIN WHOM ALL THE CURRENTS ARE ALIGNED.

SUCH A PERSON WOULD BE VERY **STRONG** AND GIFTED BY FATE.

THORN IS SUCH A PERSON. PERHAPS YOU ARE TOO.

HMM, WELL. STRONG AND GIFTED . . . THAT **IS** HARD TO DENY, BUT I STILL DON'T SEE WHY THE HOODED ONE WANTS MY SOUL - -

oh...

GRAN'MA? WHAT'S WRONG?

IT - - IT'S THE **GITCHY FEELIN'** . . . THAT **TERRIBLE** FEELING THAT MAKES YOUR HEAD SWIM AND YOUR LEGS WOBBLE! IT'S A POWERFUL **OMEN** OF BAD THINGS TO COME!

ARE YOU GONNA BE OKAY?

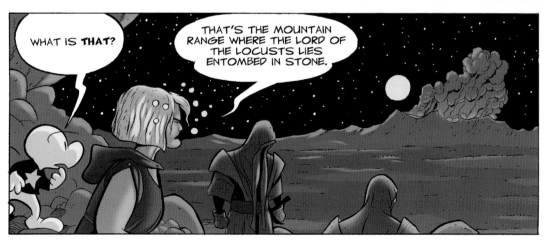

HOLY SMOKE. DID HE GET LOOSE?!

NO. BUT HE'S STIRRING.

HMM. BLOOD MOON. THAT'S A BAD SIGN.

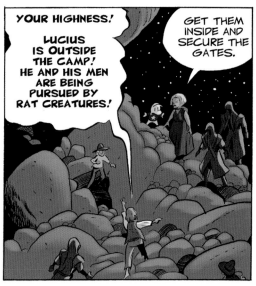

YOUR HIGHNESS! LUCIUS IS OUTSIDE THE CAMP! HE AND HIS MEN ARE BEING PURSUED BY RAT CREATURES!

GET THEM INSIDE AND SECURE THE GATES.

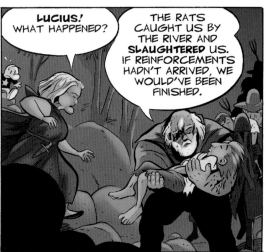

LUCIUS! WHAT HAPPENED?

THE RATS CAUGHT US BY THE RIVER AND **SLAUGHTERED** US. IF REINFORCEMENTS HADN'T ARRIVED, WE WOULD'VE BEEN FINISHED.

I SHOULD HAVE BEEN WITH YOU.

I WISH YOU HAD BEEN . . .

HERE. TAKE HIM. I DON'T KNOW IF HE'S STILL ALIVE OR NOT.

IT'S ALL MY FAULT, ROSE.

THE RAT CREATURES HAVE US COMPLETELY SURROUNDED.

CALM. BE CALM. WE MUST PREPARE FOR OUR FINAL STAND.

I JUST PRAY THAT THORN IS SAFE . . . WHEREVER SHE IS.

WOLF CALL

IT'S ALL RIGHT, CAPTAIN. WHAT IS IT, WENDELL?

GIVE HIM TO US, ROSE!

YEAH! THIS IS ALL HIS FAULT!

WHOSE FAULT, DEAR?

PHONEY BONE! "THE ONE WHO BEARS THE STAR!"

HE'S THE ONE THE RAT CREATURES ARE AFTER. THEY TORE UP THE VALLEY LOOKING FOR HIM.

YEAH! NOW THE RAT CREATURES HAVE US SURROUNDED! IF HE'S ALL THEY WANT, LET'S HAND HIM OVER!

EVEN IF HE WAS ALL THE RAT CREATURES WANTED, I WOULDN'T ADVISE GIVING THEM THE ONE THING THEY NEED TO WIN THIS WAR.

WHAT DO YOU MEAN?

OUR FRIENDS OUT THERE BELIEVE THAT THE "ONE WHO BEARS THE STAR" CAN FREE THE ANCIENT LORD OF THE LOCUSTS.

LORD OF TH--?

YOU MEAN THAT OLD FABLE ABOUT THE QUEEN OF THE DRAGONS?

OH, FER--

--THAT'S JUST A STORY! GIVE THEM PHONEY BONE AND LET 'EM TRY! WHAT CAN THE LORD OF THE LOCUSTS DO TO US?

THE LORD OF THE LOCUSTS CAN STEAL THE DREAMING THAT FLOWS THROUGH YOU.

WHY DON'T YOU TAKE THAT **STICK-EATER** MUMBO JUMBO BACK TO THE **WOODS**, YOU --

BACK OFF, WENDELL. THE ENEMY'S **OUTSIDE** THE GATES, REMEMBER?

HEY -- WHERE'S PHONEY? TH' LITTLE RAT IS **GONE!**

HE LEFT THIS.

IT'S HIS SHIRT.

SON OF A --

HE'S **ESCAPED!**

HE RAN AWAY BECAUSE YOU SCARED HIM! QUICKLY! WE HAVE TO FIND HIM!

SPREAD OUT AND SEARCH THE CAMP -- **FIND THAT BONE!** IF HE ENDS UP IN THE WRONG HANDS, IT'S GOING TO BE A REAL SHORT WAR.

HOLD IT RIGHT THERE, SQUIRT!

GRAN'MA--

WHERE DO YOU THINK **YOU'RE** GOING?

I HAD TO RUN AWAY...

HAVEN'T YOU CAUSED ENOUGH TROUBLE?

EVERYONE WAS IN **DANGER** AS LONG AS I STAYED THERE...

...I'M THE ONE THE RAT CREATURES WANT.

I THOUGHT IF I LEFT, THE REST OF YOU WOULD BE **SAFE!**

HORSE KNOBBIES!! YOU DON'T CARE ABOUT ANYBODY'S **SAFETY!** YOU WERE RUNNING AWAY...

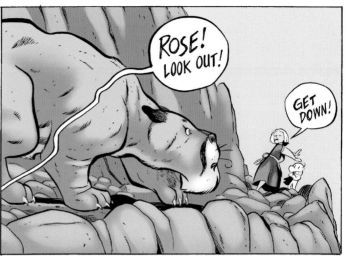

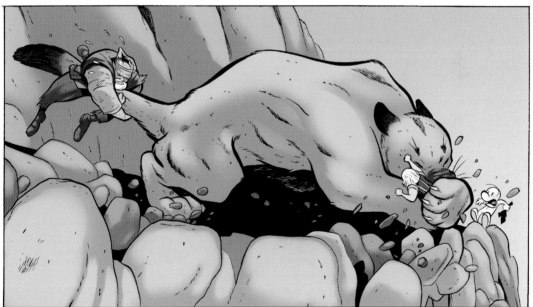

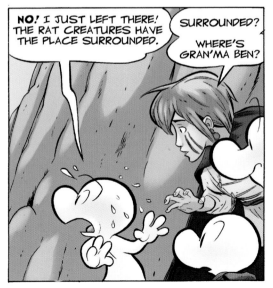

WAIT, THORN! YOU CAN'T FIGHT THAT LION-- LET'S FIND THE **DRAGON!**

FORGET IT--

THE DRAGONS WON'T HELP US -- GRAN'MA SAID THEY'VE GONE UNDERGROUND FOR GOOD.

BUT --

HEY! HEY!

IT'S ROCK JAW!

WELL!

PRINCESS THORN, I PRESUME . . .

ROCK JAW!

LOOK OUT, THORN!

KRAK!

STAND ASIDE, BONE! I NEED THE BODY.

GET AWAY!!

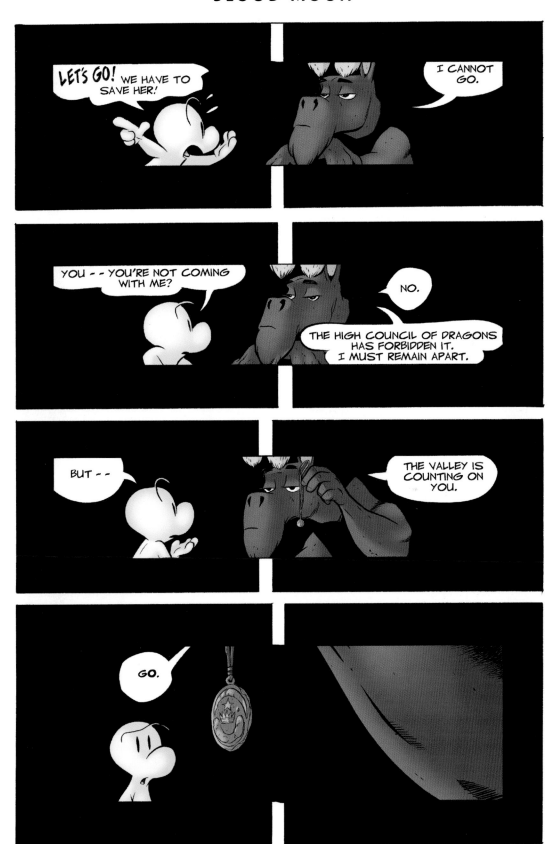

SILENCE . . .
FROM THIS MOMENT ON YOUR DESTINY IS WITH ME . . . .
TOGETHER WE WILL **FREE** OUR MASTER . . . THE ANCIENT **LORD OF THE LOCUSTS** . . . .

TAKE MY HAND, PHONCIBLE P. BONE. **TOUCH ME** . . .

FORGET IT! I AIN'T TAKIN' YOUR CREEPY HAND!

THE BLOOD MOON WAXES FULL . . . THE FORCES OF THE DREAMING . . . . AND OUR MASTER . . . ARE BEING DRAWN CLOSER TO THE STONE SURFACE THAT SEPARATES US . . .

YOU'RE **NUTS!**

IF YOU DO NOT JOIN WITH ME **WILLINGLY** . . . I AM PREPARED TO RISK THE RITUAL OF **SACRIFICE** . . . .

SACRIFICE? NOW, HOLD ON, PAL. SERIOUSLY, YOU GOT THE **WRONG GUY!** IT'S ALL A BIG **MISTAKE!**

A . . . MISTAKE . . . ? A **MISTAKE**?

DO YOU CALL **THIS** . . . A **MISTAKE**?

YOU CHASED ME ALL OVER KINGDOM COME BECAUSE OF **THAT**?!.

O BOY.

FONE BONE IS GONNA BE CRANKY WHEN HE FINDS OUT ABOUT THIS.

IT'S PHONEY'S **CAMPAIGN BALLOON**! THE ONE THAT CHASED **MISS CRAB-BONE** INTO THE RIVER!

YEAH! THE SAME BALLOON THAT GOT US RUN OUT OF BONEVILLE IN THE FIRST PLACE.

I THOUGHT YOU CAUGHT IT AND LET THE AIR OUT OF IT!

I THOUGHT **YOU** DID! IT MUST HAVE FLOATED HERE ACROSS THE DESERT.

AS SOON AS WE SAVE HIM FROM THIS SACRIFICE, LET'S **KILL** HIM!

THIS IS WHY YOU'VE BEEN SEARCHING FOR ME?! IT'S A CAMPAIGN BALLOON! THE BANNER USED TO SAY: PHONCIBLE P. BONE WILL GET YOUR **VOTE!**

I WILL NOW USE MY SCYTHE... TO CONNECT YOUR **SOUL**... DIRECTLY TO THE LIVING ROCK...

BRIAR!

THAT BONE CREATURE IS NOT A VENI-YAN-CARI. LET HIM GO!

AH, **WELCOME**, ROSE HARVESTAR... MY **SISTER**....

WHERE IS SHE, BRIAR?

I CONFESS, MY SISTER . . . THAT SEEING YOU ALIVE IS QUITE AMAZING . . .

. . . . I HAD THOUGHT YOU DIED THE SAME NIGHT **I** DID.

WHERE **IS** SHE, BRIAR?

HERE . . . IS YOUR PRECIOUS VENI-YAN-CARI . .

THE ONE **YOU** THOUGHT WOULD BE THE FUTURE RULER OF THE LAND . . .

. . . BUT SHE IS **DEAD!**

AS YOU BOTH **SHOULD** HAVE BEEN FIFTEEN YEARS AGO ON THAT MOUNTAIN PASS . . .

WHAT YOU HAVE **KILLED**, BRIAR, IS YOUR ONLY CHANCE TO FREE YOUR **MASTER** -- THE LORD OF THE LOCUSTS.

EVEN **I** CAN SEE THIS BALLOON IS NO OMEN OF **POWER** - - IT IS MERELY A SYMBOL OF **PRIDE** AND **VANITY!**

YOUR **JEALOUSY** OF THE TRUE VENI-YAN-CARI HAS BLINDED YOU -- AND YOU HAVE BADLY MISCALCULATED, MY **SISTER.**

NO...

NO, I HAVE NOT MISCALCULATED... HE **HAS** THE POWER TO FREE OUR MASTER -- HE **MUST!**

LISTEN, SIS... I ENJOY A HOSTILE TAKEOVER AS MUCH AS THE NEXT GUY, BUT FACE **FACTS!** YOU BLEW IT!

WHAT HAVE YOU **DONE,** STICK-EATER?

IT WAS THE **PRINCESS** WE NEEDED, NOT THE BONE! AND YOU HAD HER **KILLED!**

YOU HAVE BROUGHT DISGRACE UPON MY PEOPLE IN THE EYES OF THE LORD OF THE LOCUSTS...

WAIT -- DID YOU FEEL THAT?

SOME-THING MOVED DEEP IN THE EARTH!

FONE BONE! **NO!**

I'M GOING DOWN THERE!

THOOM

THOOM! hisss

THORN! ARE YOU OKAY?

I - - I THINK SO. YES.

SEE? I TOLD YOU SHE WAS STILL ALIVE!

CAN YOU WALK? WE HAVE TO GET OUT OF HERE!

YES, I'M FINE. REALLY.

ATTA GIRL!

HURRY! THIS PLACE IS FALLING APART!

ooh!

...TO BE CONTINUED.

About JEFF SMITH

JEFF SMITH was born and raised in the American Midwest and learned about cartooning from comic strips, comic books, and watching animated shorts on TV. After four years of drawing comic strips for The Ohio State University's student newspaper and co-founding Character Builders animation studio in 1986, Smith launched the comic book *BONE* in 1991. Between *BONE* and other comics projects, Smith spends much of his time on the international guest circuit promoting comics and the art of graphic novels.

More about *BONE*

An instant classic when it first appeared in the U.S. as an underground comic book in 1991, Bone has since garnered 38 international awards and sold a million copies in 15 languages. Now Scholastic's **GRAPHIX** imprint is publishing full-color graphic novel editions of the nine-book *BONE* series. Look for the continuing adventures of the Bone cousins in *Ghost Circles*.

READ
ALL
THE
BOOKS

JEFF SMITH

BONE

THE DRAGONSLAYER

JEFF SMITH

BONE

ROCK JAW
Master of the Eastern Border

SCHOLASTIC

JEFF SMITH

BONE

OLD MAN'S CAVE

SCHOLASTIC

JEFF SMITH

BONE

GHOST CIRCLES

SCHOLASTIC

JEFF SMITH

BONE

TREASURE HUNTERS

SCHOLASTIC

JEFF SMITH

BONE

CROWN OF HORNS

SCHOLASTIC

JEFF SMITH

BONE

ILLUSTRATED BY
CHARLES VESS

ROSE

SCHOLASTIC